THE TRIANGLE

MW00636403

THE TRIANGLE

Jennifer Victores

& Debbie Viguié

Published by JIV Publishing

The Triangle

Copyright © 2019 by Jennifer Victores

ISBN-13: 978-1-7343665-0-1

Published by JIV Publishing

To Valentina and Izabella. You are my inspiration. Never be afraid to chase your dreams. - JV

To Scott, the man I have loved through all time. - DV

1

Miami, 2015

Calamity always strikes when things are perfect. The answer is to never be too happy so that you can never be too miserable.
Sally White realized she had dozed off for just a moment and had dreamed of her grandmother, a wretched woman who had spent her entire life alone. She'd never understood true happiness, not the kind Sally had. As thoughts of her evaporated, Sally forced her eyes open.

She found herself staring into her husband Mark's deep, emerald green gaze. He smiled at her.

"There you are. I thought I was boring you," he teased. "Usually afterward you're the talkative one and I'm the one falling asleep."

Sally smiled and stretched. Her arms and legs were intertwined with his in the most delicious way. "You don't usually surprise me with breakfast in bed first."

"We're alone in the house. We've got to take advantage of these things while we can," he said, nuzzling her ear.

"I thought we took plenty of advantage last night." She grinned.

"With you, there's no such thing."

"I'll have to let the girls spend the weekend with my parents more often," she said, thinking of Emma and Jayne.

"Maybe it's time you and I considered going on a second honeymoon," he said, kissing her neck.

"I think we should start right now and just stay in bed all day."

He sighed as he pushed a strand of hair out of her eyes. "As wonderful as that sounds, I can't just leave Dave hanging."

"He knows how to steer the boat."

"Yeah, but it's *my* boat," Mark said. "And I'm the one who planned the fishing trip three months ago. It'd be a little rude if I didn't show up."

She gave him a lingering kiss. "You're right. I just--I don't want you to go."

"Believe me, I'm regretting it myself," he said. "Of course, you've got big plans, too. All week you've been talking about being able to go shopping without the girls. You've been saying a day all by yourself would be--what was the word?"

"Heavenly," she murmured as he nuzzled her neck again. "You're right. Let's just promise each other this won't be the last morning we get to spend together like this in the next twenty years."

"They'll be in college before that," he teased.

"Yeah. With our luck they'll be going local and we still won't have any privacy."

He kissed her. "I promise, more of this for us. Just as soon as I get back."

Reluctantly, Sally got up and dressed. The morning did remind her of the early days of their marriage, before kids and jobs and responsibilities piled up. With all of that had come some successes and a lot of joy, but sometimes she longed for the simple life they used to have.

She watched him dress, admiring the ripple of the muscles in his shoulders as he slipped on his shirt. They'd been married nearly a decade, and he was far more handsome now than he had been back then. They'd married just out of college and he'd still been a skinny, gangly kid. The broad shoulders and lean, tight muscles he had now had been nowhere in evidence.

"I love you," she said.

He turned and gave her a slow, sexy smile. "That's good, because you're never getting rid of me. It would be seriously awkward for you if you had to spend the rest of your life with someone you didn't like."

She laughed and threw a pillow at him, which he easily caught. His physique might be that of a man, but he had the same boyish smile which had first caught her attention back in ninth grade.

"I love you, too," he said. "Always and forever."

"Promise?"

"Cross my heart."

It was a ritual they'd had for years which always made her feel happy and safe.

~

They both finished dressing, and twenty minutes later they regrouped at the front door. Mark grabbed his fishing hat, a beat-up tan bucket hat dotted with fishing lures.

It was his lucky fishing hat. Mostly, it was lucky for him because Sally had bought it for him when he got the boat. He knew it was her way of supporting his fishing mania even if she didn't share it. He didn't know how he had gotten so lucky as to get a wife who was smart, beautiful, and supportive.

Sally was wearing a brilliant blue dress that matched her eyes. It was one of the ones she usually saved for special occasions.

"Wow, you look awfully fancy just to go shopping," he noted.

"Today, I'm not wearing any mom clothes. I'm just a grown woman out on the town," she said with a smirk.

He felt a sudden swift pang of jealousy and reached out, pulling her into his arms. "Promise you won't even glance at any other man while I'm gone."

"I promise," she said, a little breathlessly. "You know you're my favorite husband."

He smiled. Whenever she wanted to tease him, she'd say that. He kissed her. "I'll see you tomorrow evening."

"I'll be waiting." She pulled away and flicked his hat. "This one's getting a little worn. I should probably get you a new one."

"Nope. I'm wearing this hat forever," he said.

She rolled her eyes at him. "Have fun, and tell Dave I said hello."

"Will do."

He gave her another quick kiss and then headed out the door. As he was driving away he put down the window and winked at her with a smile. This was his way of letting Sally know he loved her. A minute later, he was on his way to the marina. It was a beautiful morning. He was sure Dave was already there, prepping the boat and wondering what was taking him so long. That was okay. Dave wasn't married. He didn't have the same morning distractions Mark did.

He thought of Sally, and before he knew it he was calling her. She picked up quickly.

"I didn't expect to be hearing from you quite this soon. Everything okay?" she asked.

"I miss you."

"I miss you, too. Of course, you've only been gone for ten minutes. Maybe you should rethink the trip."

"Believe me, I would if I could."

"I know. This is the only bonding time you and Dave get. I understand. Of course, with no one here to supervise me I may just decide to do something crazy, like buy new appliances, redo the living room…who knows what could happen."

He laughed, knowing she wouldn't do anything that extravagant out of the blue. "Tell you what. I don't care if you buy a new oven, as long as you make lasagna in it tomorrow night."

"Sure, I can pick up a frozen one at the store."

He shook his head. She always teased that she was going to do that. Her made-from-scratch lasagna was his favorite thing to eat. Usually she only made it on special occasions, but he had his fingers crossed.

"So, second honeymoon. I hear Paris is magical," he said.

4

"I thought that St. Augustine was magical," she said.

"It was a great honeymoon. If we went back there, though, we'd have to see if we couldn't convince whoever owned that mansion you loved with those amazing gardens to let us stay there for the night."

He could hear her laughing. "Yeah, we'll just stroll up, ring the doorbell, and say, 'Pardon us, but we've admired your house for years. Care to give us the tour?' I'm sure that will go over real well."

"I was thinking more of along the lines of, 'Hello, I'm an award-winning architect and I'd like to study your house for a day or two as an example of nineteenth century Floridian architecture' approach might work."

"That is a good angle. Clever," she praised him.

"Your husband can be pretty smart sometimes."

"Which one?"

"Your favorite one."

'I see. And when is my favorite husband coming home tomorrow?"

"I'll be home before dark," he assured her. "We can talk all about the second honeymoon then."

"In that case, I'll make the lasagna."

He arrived at the marina and slowly drove until his boat was in sight. He could see Dave aboard, clearly raring to go.

"You are the best," he told her. "I'm at the boat. Looks like Dave's about to burst."

"Have fun."

"I love you."

"I love you, too."

He hung up as he got out of the car. He blew a kiss in the direction of their house, another little tradition from the days when they'd only had one car and she'd had to drop him off at whatever boat he had rented space on for the day.

He grabbed his duffle bag from the trunk and watched as a teenage boy with a sharp, hawkish nose climbed out of the car next to his. Moments later, Mark was boarding his boat. It was a

5

fifty-five foot yacht named *The Guardians*.

"Hey, Dave, I saw another one of your kids in the parking lot. Had your nose. Same cheekbones, too."

Dave turned to look at him, eyes narrowing over that same large, hawkish nose as the kid in the parking lot. He gave an exaggerated sigh. "Yes, very good. By your count I'm up to how many progeny at this point?"

"Gee, I'm not sure I've kept count, but I'd say at least a hundred and twelve."

Dave smirked. "Wherever do I find the time?"

"Wow, cracking a joke like that and we're not even out of the marina! Careful, someone might hear you," Mark said, only half-teasing. Dave was a Catholic priest, and while he didn't wear the collar on fishing trips, there was always the risk that someone would recognize him and gossip about whatever he was doing or saying on his down time. Mark would never want to live with the kind of scrutiny his friend was constantly under.

"Well, then let's get out of here. I've got some real colorful things to say today."

"You're the captain."

"Be a good first mate and toss off the ropes," Dave instructed.

"Aye-aye," Mark said, saluting him and then untying the boat from the dock. "All clear, Captain."

He liked to give Dave crap, but on the boat, his friend really was the Captain. He was the one with all the navigation skills. He'd spent four years in the navy right after high school before going to seminary.

Moments later, they were leaving Miami behind and heading for their favorite fishing spot in the Keys. As soon as they were out of the marina, Mark felt the weight of stress he usually carried slip from his shoulders, and he could tell by the change in his posture that Dave felt the same way.

It was a beautiful day without a cloud in the sky and yet it wasn't too hot, as it oftentimes got. There was a light breeze which helped keep things cool. Mark breathed in deeply of the salty air. Out here on the water, it was easy to let the stress of modern life go.

That was one of the things he loved about fishing. It was simple. Fundamental. When he was out on the water fishing, he had a connection to thousands of years of ancestors who had done the same. Not a whole lot had changed, except for the boats. He had a fishing pole and the company of a friend.

"Sometimes when we're out I feel as if it's the eighteenth century," he told Dave.

The other man rolled his eyes. "I don't think either of us would want to live in the seventeen-hundreds."

"I don't know. Simpler time. Something to be said for that."

"I've got three words for you," Dave chimed back at him. "No. Internal. Plumbing."

Mark chuckled. "You would have made a terrible explorer."

"Know yourself and know your enemy and you'll be victorious in a thousand battles."

"Sun Tzu would be so proud. How did you ever survive in the navy?"

"Modern conveniences."

"So, you never had the desire to become an old-time sailor?"

"I didn't say that."

"Okay, so maybe not the eighteenth century."

A shiver suddenly danced up Mark's spine. For just a moment, the air around him felt electric, like the build-up before a storm. The skies remained clear and the seas were calm.

It's just your imagination, he lectured himself. *On such a perfect day as this, nothing could possibly go wrong.*

2

Sally had decided to put off the grocery shopping until the next morning. It was too glorious a day to waste on such a mundane activity. Instead, she decided to stroll along the shops down by South Beach. The bright colors, outrageous outfits and sparkling jewelry matched her mood. She briefly thought about calling one of her friends to come join her, but Mark was right. She'd been dreaming about alone time all week. Might as well take advantage of it.

She loved being a mom, and she loved her girls more than anything, but sometimes it was nice to have grown-up time with her husband and friends. It was also nice to occasionally be alone with her own thoughts and just be able to *be,* without having to carry on a conversation or think about the other person.

Today, the only person she had to please was herself.

She strolled leisurely, nodding and smiling to people, but that was the extent of the interaction required of her. At one point as she was shopping she found a ridiculously loud aloha-style shirt with fish all over it and briefly thought about buying it for Mark. It suited his style, and the crazy thing was, he would no doubt wear it somewhere inappropriate just to embarrass her.

At least she'd known what she was getting herself into from Day One. He was an avid fisherman when they'd met. His grandfather used to take him all the time when he was a little kid. Mark had fished all up and down the coast of Florida. When they started dating in eleventh grade, he'd told her she was the only thing he liked more than fishing. A year later, when he blew off a fishing tournament to take her to prom, she'd finally believed him. If that wasn't true love, nothing was.

She decided against purchasing the shirt and kept walking. She walked into a funky little bookshop that had practically become an institution in the area. They were famous for having speakers and writers coming in to visit on a weekly basis. An easel up front had a poster with a large picture of a dark-haired woman posed in that thoughtful, chin-on-hand pose in which so many authors seemed to like to be photographed. The lighting shining on her was dramatic, giving rise to a sense of shadow and mystery. The name *Janis Coleman* was splashed across the middle of the poster. There was more, but Sally didn't pay attention. Mystery wasn't really her genre, and besides, it wasn't as if she had time to read with her busy life.

She perused a couple of the tables up front, fantasizing about what it would be like to have time to read again. She used to love it. There was a reprint of an old book written about the early days of Florida which they stocked mostly for tourists. She picked up a romance novel and glanced at it for a moment, quickly perusing the back cover before putting it down again. Who needed to read about other couples' happily-ever-afters when she already had the most romantic husband in the world?

Real life beat fairy tales every day of the week.

~

It was early evening and all Mark's cares seemed to have melted away in the twilight. He wasn't worried about the complicated redesign he was in the middle of for the new bank building downtown, nor was he concerned over the two deals his company had been working to close for the last month. Instead, he was simply relaxing, watching the sun slowly sinking toward the horizon and daydreaming about Sally.

"What are you thinking about?" Dave asked with a curious smile.

"My wife."

His grin widened. "Must be nice to be married."

"It is, and not only for the particular reason currently on my mind."

"Pervert."

"Prude."

The easy banter came from years of close friendship. Dave had once told him Mark was the only one of his friends who hadn't started treating him differently once he'd become a priest. He knew the other man valued that. A priest needed a close friend as much as the next man, someone with whom he could just blow off steam and not worry that he'd be judged.

It had been a good day so far. They'd landed half a dozen beautiful fish, which they'd cleaned and stored in the refrigerators made for just that purpose.

"If we do half as well tomorrow," Dave pointed out, "we won't need a miracle to be feasting on fish for the rest of the year."

"Oh, man. You maybe, but not me. Sally starts twitching if she has to eat fish more than once a week."

The priest chuckled. "I'm happy to take that burden off your hands. More fish for me, then."

"Somehow I didn't think it would be a problem."

Mark stood up. "I'm going to give Sally a quick call, just to touch base with her and see how the shopping went."

"Now, there's a surprise," the other man said with a laugh. "You wanting to speak to your honey."

Mark rolled his eyes at his friend and made his way down to the master bedroom. He called Sally as soon as he was inside. As the phone rang, he listened to the static on the line. To his surprise, the call went straight to her voicemail and her outgoing message came through a bit garbled. He wondered if the boat was situated in a bad spot.

"Hey, babe, it's me. I miss you. I love you. Goodbye."

He hung up, frustrated that he hadn't actually been able to speak to her. An intense wave of longing he couldn't explain suddenly washed over him. He waited a couple of minutes to see if she'd call him back.

Finally, he left the room to rejoin Dave on deck. The sun had set and darkness was closing in fast. He found his friend standing next to the railing, staring up at the sky and frowning.

"What's wrong, captain?"

Dave turned to him, his brow furrowed. "I don't see the moon."

"I thought this would have been something your dad taught you when you were a little tyke. Just because you can't see the moon doesn't mean it's not there," Mark said, trying to recapture his earlier good mood.

Dave just scowled harder. "I'm not joking. It's supposed to be nearly full tonight."

"I'm sure it is. It must be hiding behind some clouds. It will show itself soon enough."

"But there weren't any clouds earlier."

"Well, there must be now. Either that, or you read the wrong day on the calendar. Don't worry about it. With our running lights on, other ships can see us for miles."

"I guess," Dave said, sounding more worried than he usually did, especially considering this was supposed to be a vacation for them.

"On the other hand, if you've got some kind of an inside line on the date for the end of the world, I'd appreciate a heads-up. After all, it could be bad for business."

His quip had the desired effect. It broke the tension that had suddenly seemed to descend upon them.

"Arrogant prick," Dave muttered.

"Superstitious fool," he countered.

They settled into deck chairs in a comfortable silence, listening to the gentle lap of small waves against the boat. In a short while, Mark felt himself being lulled to sleep.

"I think I'm going to turn in."

"Okay. I'll probably head to bed in a few minutes myself," Dave muttered, his eyes fixed on the dark water.

Mark made his way back downstairs, convinced that as soon as he slipped between the sheets he'd be dead to the world. It sounded like a pretty good idea with the boat rocking him to sleep like a babe in a cradle.

~

Sally was soaking in her bathtub, enjoying the penetrating warmth of the bubble bath as she stretched out her leg and shoulder muscles. It had been such a long time since she had an evening all to herself that she stayed in longer than she originally intended, savoring both the warmth and the quiet.

When she got out, she changed into her comfiest pajamas and flopped down on the bed. She sighed happily and glanced around the bedroom. She loved this room so much. Mark had been the architect, and they had fulfilled their dream of designing their own home. Everything about it reminded her of him.

Her eyes drifted to the ceiling. There, in the crown molding, were two intertwined hearts he had put in as a signature piece. It represented the two of them and the love which kept them together.

She reached for her phone, feeling the need to call him and hear his voice. She was surprised when her call went straight to voicemail. She sighed in frustration and hung up, deciding to text him instead.

Love you.

She put the phone down on her nightstand and debated what to watch on television before falling asleep. Instead, she found herself dropping off into sleep.

She was awoken by the sudden chime of her phone. She picked it up and saw Mark's reply.

Love u 2.

Miss you.

It took longer than usual, but his reply finally came back.

Miss u more. Tried calling earlier, left voicemail.

In tub. No voicemail.

I left one, he insisted.

12

I'll probably get it later. How's Dave?

Good.

The fish?

Excellent.

I still have fish in freezer from last time, she reminded him, hoping he would take the hint.

Most r Dave's.

Good. Can't wait 4 tomorrow night.

Lasagna's going 2 b good.

She sent an emoji with the tongue sticking out.

What are u wearing?

Nothing.

Really?

No. Pajamas.

I knew the other was 2 good 2 b true.

What are you wearing? she asked.

Guess.

What do I get if I guess right?

There was a lengthy pause and then his next text came in.

Gotta run. POS.

She laughed. For most people that would mean Parents Over Shoulder. For them, it meant Priest Over Shoulder.

She sent him a heart emoji and then put her phone down, snuggling into the coolness of the bedsheets and drifting into a deep sleep.

~

Mark was surprised when Dave showed up in his room unexpectedly. The other man didn't look right, and something about his sudden appearance made the hair on the back of Mark's neck stand on end.

"What's wrong?" he asked, sitting up and swinging his legs over the edge of the bed.

"I don't know. Nothing, I guess."

"Okay, from the look on your face, it is definitely not

13

nothing. So, I'm going to ask you again. What's going on?"

"It's…I don't know. I've just got this weird feeling."

"Weird in what way?"

"Like something isn't right, you know?"

Mark sucked in his breath. "Is this like the weird feeling you had back in 2001?"

He was the only person who knew Dave had suffered nightmares about the attack on the World Trade Center two weeks before it happened. Dave wasn't alone. Thousands of other people had also had the same experience. But it was something Dave really didn't like talking about.

"Yes. No. I don't know."

"That's good enough for me to take seriously. What do you think is wrong?"

"If I could put it into words, I would," Dave said, sounding supremely frustrated. "Tonight, the ocean feels different somehow."

"You think a storm is coming?"

"I've checked and rechecked the forecasts. There's nothing."

"Let's go up on deck," Mark suggested.

Dave nodded. "I'm sorry. I didn't want to wake you, given that it's so late."

Mark shook his head. "Never worry about waking me up. Besides, it's only…" He tapped his phone to bring up the time. He blinked when he saw the numbers. "Seven minutes past midnight? That can't be right. I haven't been in this room more than half an hour."

"You probably just drifted off to sleep for a while," Dave said as he turned and headed out of the room.

Mark shook his head to clear it and then followed the other man up the stairs. The first thing he noticed on deck was that the night was pitch black. Weird, considering what Dave had said about the moon supposedly being nearly full.

But as Mark had pointed out earlier, there was no reason to worry. So what if he couldn't see the moon or stars. They had to

14

be behind a thick cloud bank. There were no other ships anywhere around, which meant the only light was coming from their boat.

There was no longer a breeze. The air was completely still. He had to strain to even hear the quiet lapping of waves against the hull. The vast emptiness was beautiful, but also more than a bit unnerving. He could understand why it was spooking David.

"It feels as if we're the only two people in the world," Mark said in hushed tones. He didn't know why he was speaking in a whisper, but somehow it felt appropriate--necessary, even.

"I know. I come on these trips specifically for the peace and quiet, but this is a little too--"

"Quiet?"

"Yeah."

They stood for several minutes, looking around and concentrating on what was before them. Mark found that his field of vision was very limited. He could see water where the lights from the boat shone on it, but even just a few feet out, everything was utter blackness.

Mark shook his head. "I think our imaginations are running away with us. We've been stuck in the noisy, busy city for too long."

"Maybe you're right," Dave said slowly.

"Even if we wanted to head in early, it's just so dark out here I don't think it would be a good idea."

Dave nodded.

They stood there for a couple more minutes in silence. If it was possible, the sound of the waves grew even fainter. He wondered if this was what going deaf felt like.

Next to him, Dave snapped his fingers, the sudden sound booming into the darkness.

Mark jumped. "Why did you do that?"

"To test my hearing."

Mark realized Dave was also straining to hear any sound, which was more than a little creepy. He wasn't sure if that made him feel better or worse. "Do we normally see ships out here at night?" he asked.

"I was wondering the same thing. We always turn in early, though, so I don't know for certain. I've never heard a ship at night before, but that doesn't mean anything."

Mark clapped a hand on Dave's shoulder. "Okay, enough of spooking each other out. Those fish tomorrow morning won't catch themselves. I'm going to go get some rest. You should, too."

Dave gave a slight nod.

Mark turned to the stairs leading down to the cabins. Dave was still standing outside, rock solid and staring into the distance.

Inside his cabin, Mark picked up his phone, thinking he might finish his text conversation with Sally. When he glanced at the time, though, he was just as shocked as he'd been earlier.

How on earth did I just spend two hours on deck without knowing it?

3

Sally jolted wide awake. She sat up, panting as she tried to catch her breath. She was sweating profusely, and her heart was racing. She realized that she must have been having a nightmare, even though she couldn't remember anything like that. She reached for her phone, her first instinct to call Mark. He always knew how to calm her right down. She hesitated, though, when she saw that it was just before five.

She sat for a moment, finger hovering over his name, while she tried to calm herself down. Mark rarely got any downtime because of how busy his work kept him. He was almost certainly asleep, and she decided not to wake him. After all, there was nothing wrong.

She sat there for a moment, rubbing her arms and thinking about Mark. She wished he was home with her, but knew she was overreacting. He would be home in only twelve more hours.

There in the dark and silence, though, twelve hours sounded like an eternity to wait.

Stop being so needy, she silently lectured herself. *He'll be home in your arms soon.*

She took a deep breath, laid back down and went back to sleep.

~

Mark didn't know what woke him. All he knew was that one moment he was sound asleep and the next he was wide awake. He waited a moment, blinking against the darkness of the cabin.

He turned his head toward the hallway where there were safety lights along the baseboards, and narrowed his eyes to see better.

As he watched, one of them flickered and went out. He had never seen anything like that happen before. The light on the opposite side of the hall appeared to glow brighter for a moment before it, too, flared then went suddenly dark. A moment later the remaining lights went out, all at the same time.

Mark sat up and swung his legs over the edge of the bed. Something was definitely wrong. He could feel it in his gut.

"Dave!" he shouted.

In the pitch darkness, he opened the drawer next to the bed, fumbling for the flashlight he kept in there. When he clicked on the light it was nearly blinding. He heard running steps, followed by a crash and Dave cursing in Latin.

Mark stood up, crossed to the doorway and shined his flashlight down the hall. Dave was picking himself up off the floor, his body twisted in pain as he leaned against the wall for balance. He tried to stand and then let out a strangled yelp.

"What is it?" Mark asked as he moved toward him.

"My foot. I think I broke it. I couldn't see the wall and slammed right into it."

"The lights burned out all at once," Mark said, putting an arm around Dave's waist. Together, they limped to Mark's room and got Dave down on the small chair in the room.

"That's weird," Dave said through gritted teeth.

"Tell me about it," Mark muttered. He went and grabbed the First Aid kit and brought it back into the room.

He shined the light on Dave's foot and could see that it was already swelling and changing color. "Yeah, it looks like you broke it," he said, angry with himself for shouting in panic at the other man.

"It's not your fault," Dave said, as though reading his mind. "My foot is killing me. Please tell me you've got something in there for pain."

"Aspirin."

"You've got to be kidding me," he said through gritted

18

teeth.

Mark stopped and thought for a long moment. "Remember the trip we took after I had the dental surgery? The doctor had given me some really strong prescription pain killers."

"Yeah."

Mark headed over to the toiletry bag he kept on the boat. "As I recall, you gave me this long lecture on being careful to not get addicted and badgered me until I stopped taking them— even though I was still in pain, I might add."

He rummaged through the bag and found the prescription bottle. He grabbed it along with a bottle of water that was on the counter. "You remember that?"

"Just shut up and give them to me," Dave groaned as he reached for the water.

The flashlight Mark was holding dimmed suddenly, as though the battery had drained.

"Don't do this to me now," he said, smacking the flashlight against his palm a couple of times. The light burned brighter for a moment then sputtered and died, plunging them back into darkness.

Mark swore loudly.

"I heard that," Dave said.

"You're in too much pain. You don't know what you heard," Mark said, trying for a tiny bit of levity. His own stress levels were spiking out of control.

There was a sudden thud as something hit the hull of the ship.

"I heard *that*," Dave said. "And it didn't sound good."

"So, did I," Mark muttered, silently agreeing with his friend's assessment.

"That wasn't a wave."

"I know."

There was a long moment of silence.

"Maybe it was just a school of fish accidentally hitting the boat," Dave said, sounding as if he was trying to convince himself.

"Or maybe it was something larger purposely hitting the boat," Mark suggested, struggling to calm his imagination, which was going into overdrive despite his best efforts.

"That wasn't meant to make me feel better."

"Me either."

The boat rocked and it almost threw Mark off balance. He struggled to regain his footing.

"Can I have the pills before you drop them?" Dave asked.

"It's so dark I can't see anything, including you. You don't want me to lose them, right?"

"Shake the bottle and I'll find it."

Mark shook the bottle. The rattling of the pills inside sounded incredibly loud to him. Moments later, Dave's hand closed around his and then took the bottle from him.

"We have other lanterns and flashlights on this boat," Dave said after gulping down a pain pill with water. "And I know I've got extra batteries somewhere. I just can't think of where they are at the moment. My phone's got a flashlight app, but we need to conserve our batteries for those, just in case."

Just in case.

Those words felt like a slap across Mark's face.

Just in case they were stranded. Just in case Dave was a lot worse off than they both thought. Just in case whatever was out there hit the boat a lot harder.

"It's my boat. You would think I'd remember where I put everything," Mark said, getting frustrated with himself. The truth was, the unease which had been growing in him for the last several hours had reached epic proportions and he could barely contain it. Something wasn't right. He didn't relish the idea of stumbling around the boat alone in the dark, trying to find lights that might or might not work.

Dave chuckled suddenly. "Of course, one of us could just flip on the light switch in this room. Then we wouldn't have to worry about finding flashlights."

Mark felt like an idiot. He put it up to his creeping paranoia and his fear that all the lights in the boat had failed, not just the ones in the hall.

He cursed under his breath.

"I heard that, too."

"I promise I'll serve whatever penance you want later. The light switch is on the wall behind you, to your right and up a bit."

He could hear Dave's hand sliding along the wall as he searched for the switch. The sound was eerie in the dark and sent another chill down Mark's spine.

This whole thing was stupid. Any second Dave would turn on the light and they'd have a good laugh about what idiots they'd both been, being afraid of the dark. Then they'd bandage up Dave's foot and head for home.

"Found it. I've flipped it repeatedly but nothing's happening," Dave said a few seconds later, his voice grim.

"You don't think that we've lost electrical for the whole ship, do you?" Mark asked, his anxiety returning in full force.

"I was really hoping you weren't going to ask that."

"Well, I'm asking."

"There's one way to find out."

Mark took a deep breath. "One of us has to go up to the wheelhouse."

"Normally, I'd volunteer. I am the captain, after all. Given the circumstances, though…"

"Yeah, I get it. Just watch your feet. I don't want to accidentally break the other one tripping over you."

"If I could watch my feet we wouldn't be in this predicament."

"I'm glad you're still finding humor in all this," Mark said as he edged forward, blindly aiming for the doorway.

A hand clamped down on his arm, startling him.

"Move a bit to your left," Dave murmured.

Mark did as instructed. He reached out his left arm, feeling for the door. His fingers finally brushed against the door frame. He gripped it tightly and moved forward with more confidence as Dave let go of his other arm.

21

Thunk!

Something hit the side of the hull again, making the boat rock.

The hair on the back of Mark's neck stood on end.

"I didn't hear that," he whispered, wishing that saying it out loud would somehow make it true.

"I definitely didn't hear it, either," Dave said, his tone foreboding.

"Glad we're agreed."

"Be careful."

Mark didn't respond. A cold sweat had broken out on his forehead. The last thing he wanted to do was go topside to find out what was going on. He wanted to sit tight in the room and wait for dawn.

If it comes.

He tried to shove the thought out of his head, but it persisted. Over and over, he kept thinking about how dark it had been the evening before. Dave had kept mentioning the missing moon. It was as if they'd fallen into some black hole in the middle of the ocean.

He should have at least checked his phone to see the time. For all he knew, dawn was just a few minutes off and he was walking around in the dark for no good reason.

He put his hands on the walls on either side of the hallway and headed for the stairs. Then again, it was possible that he hadn't been asleep long and dawn was still a long way off.

He came to the break in the wall he'd been looking for. The stairs would take him topside to the deck, and from there he could climb up another short set of stairs to where the steering wheel, radio and navigation equipment were located. He tried not to think about the next set of stairs, though. For the moment, he just needed to safely navigate this set.

He tightly gripped both handrails as he walked up, deliberately setting each foot before trusting his full weight to it. When he finally emerged on deck, he found everything was just as dark as it had been down below. The air was as still as it had been earlier, too. He'd been hoping for a breeze to fan his face, but there was none.

He stood for a moment in the doorway, swiveling his head around and staring into the night sky, trying to find even the slightest glimmer of light. There must still be thick cloud cover, because there was not the least bit of light from the moon or stars. It unnerved him that in the pitch black, he couldn't tell the sea from the sky. His eyes were straining, trying to differentiate one from the other, but had no luck. In the back of his mind, he kept thinking that he should at least be able to see the water close up against the boat.

After a few moments, it finally dawned on him why he couldn't.

The ship's running lights were off.

4

Mark sucked in his breath. What if they had lost *all* their electrical systems? He needed to climb up to the wheelhouse and check up there. In the inky blackness, though, he knew it would be dangerous to navigate up the ladder and perch on top.

Especially if something hits the ship again, he thought.

He tried to tell himself that it was probably just a large fish that couldn't discern the boat's presence. With the ship's lights off, maybe they were crashing into it.

That would have to be a seriously large fish to have made those heavy bumps.

His mind instantly conjured an image of a shark. Several different species of sharks called these waters home, including tigers, hammerheads and makos, among others. He forced himself to take a deep breath. Most sharks were content to let people well enough alone unless there was prey nearby.

You are not going to fall in the water and get eaten by a shark, he silently scolded himself.

He had never been afraid of sharks until his grandfather took him on a fishing trip to California. There, he had witnessed a Great White feeding frenzy firsthand and it had stuck with him all these years. Even though whites didn't swim in these waters, whenever he thought of sharks now, he thought of them.

"Thanks, Grandfather," he whispered as a shiver went down his spine.

The night caught his words and shoved them right back at him, as though trying to ram them down his throat. He had the unnerving sensation that he was trapped inside a tiny, black box which he couldn't see. It felt as if his voice was carrying no more than a couple of inches past his lips.

It's like being in a tomb, he thought as he felt panic beginning to swell again. *What if Dave and I are dead? What if something happened while we were sleeping?*

He slapped himself hard across the face, both to feel the pain as a way to reassure himself that he was alive and awake and to focus his attention on something other than his mounting fear. The sting of the skin on his cheek did just that.

He grit his teeth and moved forward, feeling his way to the ladder and resolutely making his way up. When he reached the top, he extended his hand toward the captain's chair, grabbing the back of it and using it to guide him to the controls.

It only took a moment to realize everything was completely dead. He wasn't sure how that was even possible. The system was pretty much self-contained, and they couldn't possibly have done anything to drain the batteries down this far. He wasn't sure why the generator wasn't taking care of the problem. They had back-up parts on board, but that would have to wait for daylight when he could see what he was doing and Dave could oversee it all.

It's my boat. One of these days I should learn to pilot the thing, he thought, angry with himself. He hated feeling helpless.

The truth was, as much as he enjoyed the boat, it was more of a means to an end. What he really loved was fishing out in the middle of nowhere with no other boats or fishermen to bother him. His grandfather had taught him to treasure the peace and isolation.

Well, he certainly had that now.

His grandfather had also never let him drive the boat, a much simpler craft than the one he was currently on. His parents had sold the *Solitude* after his grandfather died, even though Mark had begged them not to.

His overriding fear had turned to frustration as he made his way back down the ladder. With his feet firmly on the deck, he breathed deeply. He felt his way to the stairs leading down to the living quarters. Depending on how bad Dave's foot looked when they were able to assess it in the light, they might need to call the Coast Guard for assistance. The last thing they needed was to dawdle if he needed to get to a hospital.

He was about to take the first step down the stairs when something hit the boat hard. It threw him sideways and only his grip on the doorframe kept him from pitching into the darkness. The sound had been frightening down below, but up above, it was absolutely chilling.

It couldn't be another boat, because they wouldn't be running blind. Even the kinds of ships that might wouldn't on a night like this. Besides, whatever had hit them seemed to have done it below the water line.

From down below, he heard an odd, tinny sound which rose and fell slowly, like someone talking very slowly through one of those tin-can string phones he'd made as a kid. Though it didn't sound like his voice, it had to be coming from Dave.

Mark hurried down the staircase, keeping a firm grip on the handrails in case the boat was struck again. It was still pitch black below and he carefully traced his way through the dark.

"Dave?" he called, unable to keep the anxiety out of his tone.

"Are you okay?" Dave's hoarse voice came from just a few feet in front of him.

"Yeah."

"Thank the good Lord. I've been shouting for you the last fifteen minutes and you didn't answer. I was trying to figure out how I was going to search the boat for you in the dark without being able to walk."

"You've been calling for fifteen minutes?" Mark asked.

"Yeah. Since right after that last impact on the hull."

"That was less than a minute ago," Mark said, his heart starting to pound.

"No, dude. I guarantee you, I've yelled myself hoarse," Dave said, his voice definitely sounding that way. "It's been at least a quarter of an hour. Maybe more."

Mark finally made it into the room and groped around until he found the edge of the bed.

26

"Something really strange is going on. It's still pitch black out there. No moon. No stars. All of our electrical is unresponsive. And something--I have no idea what--appears to be attacking us."

Dave was silent for long enough that Mark finally asked, "You still with me? You didn't pass out on me, did you?"

"No, although as bad as my foot hurts, that would be a mercy," Dave responded. "I'm just thinking. First off, I don't think anything is attacking us. I think it would have sunk us by now if it was. More likely we're in some migration lane for a pod of whales or dolphins or something."

"Dolphins have sonar. I can't imagine them running into the boat no matter how dark it is."

"Fine," Dave snapped. "You're the fish guy. I'm the boat guy. I'm telling you that this boat, as beautiful as she is, couldn't sustain a real attack by--*what*? Another ship? A mysterious something or other? I don't think the bogeyman's after us."

Mark took a deep breath. He wanted to correct Dave and tell him that dolphins were mammals not fish. He could tell the other man was in a lot of pain, though, and it was clearly not the time to be argumentative. *Don't do it*, he told himself.

"Mammals," Mark burst out.

"What?"

"Dolphins are mammals, not fish."

"Jerk face."

"Dumbass."

Dave chuckled slightly. "Guess I deserve that one. Okay, as soon as it's light, we'll take a look and see what's wrong with her. At the very least, we can get the radio working and call the Coast Guard to come help us out."

"You suggested it, not me."

"Fine. Yes. Uncle. I'll admit I may need help. My foot hurts like… a very, very hot place right now, even with the pain pills."

"It can't be that bad. If it was, you'd still be swearing in

Latin."

"Ah, Father Montoya, God rest his soul. That man taught me everything I know about Latin obscenities."

"One of these days I'll make you teach me," Mark said.

"So you can understand what I'm saying and give me a hard time about it? I think not."

"We could use the cell to call right now. We've been anchored all night in the same spot, so by the time the sun starts rising the cavalry should be getting here to rescue us."

"Great. The cavalry. Army guys never lose a chance to lord it over navy guys, especially if they catch one helpless at sea."

Dave snickered at his own joke.

"How many of those pain killers did you take?" Mark asked.

"I don't know, but they're wearing off."

"Already? They should really just be starting to kick in," Mark said, concern flooding him. "You only took them a little while ago. You have to wait at least four-to-six hours before you can take any more, dude."

He groaned. "How long has it been?"

"Let me look," Mark said, feeling for his phone. His hand finally wrapped around it and he stared at the display in shock. "Dave? It's eight a.m.," he finally croaked, barely able to get the words out.

"That's not possible," Dave said, anxiety clear in his voice. "The sun should have risen over an hour ago."

"Maybe there's something wrong with my phone. I'm not getting any bars," Mark said.

"Take it up on deck," Dave suggested. "And turn it off and on again. It's got to be glitching. It couldn't be eight in the morning. If you get a signal, call the Coast Guard. We need to get out of here before things get any crazier."

"Okay," Mark said. He rose unsteadily to his feet and shoved the phone in his pocket so he'd have both hands free to navigate topside.

"Be careful," Dave said somberly.

"Yeah."

He'd made it halfway down the hall when he decided to spend some of the battery power of his phone by using the flashlight function. For a second after he opened the app, he thought it was going to crash. He held his breath. Finally, the light flickered, and the beam came on.

He angled it downward and then hurried through the hall and up the stairs. Far off in the distance, he could hear the rumble of thunder which served to hasten his steps. A storm was the last thing they needed at the moment. He had to get help before it arrived. He glanced at his phone to see if there was any change. But no--he still wasn't getting any bars.

He'd had service the night before. Why didn't he now? He turned his phone off and then back on. It seemed to take even longer to boot up than usual, but he chalked that up to his anxiety. He shifted his weight impatiently from foot to foot as he waited. Finally, his phone came back up.

No service.

He wanted to toss his phone into the sea out of frustration. Instead he forced himself to shove it back in his pocket. He decided to go back down and get Dave's phone. Maybe he'd have a better shot with it.

The hair on his arms suddenly raised.

The air changed.

Something was different.

Suddenly, a bolt of lightning shot out of the sky and hit the water about twenty feet off the stern of the boat. It struck with a huge crack that felt and sounded like an earthquake and nearly knocked him over. The air instantly smelled like ozone and he could feel the electricity in the air.

All of that was startling, but it was nothing compared to what the overwhelming brightness from the lightning bolt had revealed. In that one moment of intense, blazing light which had hurt his eyes, he had seen the ocean for a quarter of a mile out.

There was a massive wall of water over a hundred feet tall headed straight for the boat.

5

Sally smiled with pleasure as she loaded the groceries into the trunk. Not too much longer now before the love of her life would be back and she couldn't wait. She returned her now-empty cart to the cart corral and then stopped and texted Mark before she got in the car.

Just bought the frozen lasagna!

She laughed to herself. She had all the ingredients for her from-scratch lasagna in the trunk. She also had purchased a small frozen lasagna. She planned on having the empty box out on the counter when he came home, just to tease him. She couldn't wait to see the look on his face when he discovered the empty box and again when he realized she was actually making her own. She'd arranged to pick up the girls from her parents' house after dinner. *Well* after dinner—and dessert. She was hoping to enjoy a little more alone-time before the world came crashing in on her again.

She loved her daughters more than anything, but the morning before had been so nice that she was hoping for just a little bit more adult time. She'd even bought a new negligee the day before in anticipation of the evening.

She got in the car and smiled as she headed for home.

Tonight's going to be a night to remember.

~

Mark shouted at the top of his lungs and staggered down the stairs as fast as he could. He raced down the hallway, not caring if he hit the wall in the dark.

"What is it?" Dave yelled.

"Tsunami!" Mark shouted before running into the side of the bed. He tripped and sprawled across it, grunting in pain. "Hurry! Grab onto something!"

As he gripped the bedframe, he heard Dave burst into rapid prayer and he knew they had no chance of living through this. The wave was going to shatter the ship into a million pieces, and them along with it. He reached into his pocket, grabbing for his cell phone, desperately wanting to talk to Sally in his last moments.

His mind screamed at him that there was no time. He vaguely remembered he had no service, but he couldn't stop himself from trying. He was about to die and he needed to hear her voice, tell her he loved her one last time.

Any second, the wave would hit them.

All around them, a low growl arose, building in strength until he could no longer hear Dave praying. The wind howled, clawing at the inside of his mind. He squeezed his eyes shut.

Something hit the ship and it began to shake violently. He lost hold of his phone as he struggled to keep from being flung about the cabin.

Then just as suddenly as it had started, it was all over.

Mark slowly opened his eyes. Light was streaming in through the window and he blinked as he tried to focus. He glanced around and saw Dave picking himself up off the floor and climbing back into the chair. The priest's face was ashen, whether from terror or pain, Mark couldn't tell.

"What happened?" Mark finally asked, his voice raspy and his pulse uneven.

Dave shook his head. "I don't know what that was, but it wasn't a tsunami."

"We're lucky to be alive."

"No--we *shouldn't* be alive."

"God must like one of us. I think it's me," Mark said as relief coursed through him.

Dave pinned him with his gaze. "Something happened just now. And I'm telling you that whatever it was, it wasn't natural."

The sudden sick twisting in his own gut substantiated the other man's opinion. Dave was right. Something *was* wrong. He could feel it, but he couldn't explain it.

"I don't know," he finally admitted.

"Let's get the ship powered up," Dave said. He stood, his face scrunching up in pain, but he resolutely headed out the door, hopping on his one good foot while he kept the other from touching the ground.

Mark had never had an experience he couldn't explain. He knew Dave had, and he believed him, but this was just so far beyond anything he'd ever known. He couldn't even attempt to categorize how he was feeling. He wasn't even sure what he was *thinking*. It felt like a rush of images, a mass of data, information suddenly bombarding him, just waiting to crush him.

Just like the lightning had revealed the wave.

"I'm going to need your help once I get up the stairs," Dave called. "I can't do this myself. Not with this bad foot. We need to get the old girl home, and the sooner, the better."

"Coming," Mark said. *The sooner the better* was right.

He stood up and took a quick glance around, looking for his phone. He didn't know where it had landed when the wave hit them. From the sound of it, Dave was already halfway up the stairs. He gave up the search for the moment and hurried to help the other man.

~

Sally sighed as she hung up the phone. She had tried calling Mark. She'd wanted to tease him a little more about the frozen lasagna. It had gone to voicemail, though.

After she put the groceries away, she opened the freezer and stared at the remains of his last fishing trip. There were still half a dozen packages of fish filets all wrapped up nice and neat. If he brought much home this time, she'd have to make room by throwing out some of the old ones, not that she'd mind.

For a moment, she considered doing it right then, but she didn't want to stink up the trash can prematurely.

"Temporary reprieve," she told the packets as she closed the freezer door.

She got out one of her larger pots, filled it halfway with water and set it on a back burner to boil. Then she grabbed a frying pan and dumped the raw hamburger into it. She was going to make two lasagnas and freeze one. Mark's birthday was in three weeks, and she'd be shocked if he wanted anything other than his favorite lasagna to celebrate. Sometimes, predictable was a good thing. Getting to kill two birds was also a very good thing.

She glanced at the clock a few minutes later as she dropped lasagna noodles into the boiling water. Mark and Dave were probably getting in the last of their fishing before they'd have to head home.

~

It was with a sigh of relief that Mark heard the voice of the Coast Guard come on over the radio. Thankfully, they had managed to restore power to the ship. Dave nodded his head as he briefed the Coast Guard on their situation.

"We're heading for home port now," Dave said.

After the call was over, Mark looked at him. "Are you sure you're fit to drive?"

Dave was in the captain's chair and they'd managed to get his broken foot propped up a bit. He appeared distinctly uncomfortable, but his eyes were clear and alert. He must not have taken a second dose of painkillers.

"Yes. In the time it would take them to get out here and get back, we could have made it home and I would be in the ER already. I don't know about you, but I've had a little too much excitement on this fishing trip and I just want to get back as soon as possible."

"Agreed," Mark said fervently.

The boat began to move forward, her prow slicing through the water. Mark felt a tremendous surge of relief and for the first time in over twelve hours, he felt like he could breathe. The sun was high in the sky and all the darkness of the night before had vanished. It had left its mark, however, and several lingering questions remained--questions Dave was clearly as loathe to discuss as he was.

When we came up on deck, why was everything dry?

That had been the first and biggest question on his mind, after how they could possibly have survived such an event. After being hit by the tsunami, everything on the boat should have been drenched, if not decimated. Instead everything had been dry as a bone.

As if it never happened.

But it *had* happened. He *knew* it had.

At least, something had certainly happened. That something had tossed the ship pretty violently.

"You know, a lot of old timers have some pretty strange stories about this area," Dave said casually.

"Yeah?"

"Uh-huh. Plenty of strange stories. Things that don't seem… natural."

"I guess we're going to end up as two of those old timers then, huh?" Mark tried to grin and keep his tone light, but knew he'd only succeeded in a grimace at best.

Dave shook his head slowly, deliberately. "Not me. I don't have a story to tell, other than this broken foot."

He looked pointedly at Mark, clearly waiting for him to say something.

Mark frowned. "You don't want to tell anyone what happened last night and this morning?"

"Not especially. People can get a bit weird when you have experiences they haven't and you talk about it in front of them, especially when they are as inexplicable as what we encountered."

34

Mark knew Dave's parents had been less than kind when Dave had revealed to them his prophetic vision when he was younger. He was probably hoping to avoid exposing himself to more ridicule, particularly given his current position. As a priest, he had a reputation to uphold.

"Don't worry. The only person I'd tell is Sally, and I'm seriously debating that. I don't usually like to keep anything from her, but, in this case, it might be better for me to remain mum."

"Why?"

"If I tell her, I doubt she'll let me go on any more fishing trips. Ever."

"Won't *let* you?"

"You don't know what it's like to be married, man. Wives can make your life miserable if they don't want you to do something. And if I tell her about this, she might even think I'm losing my mind."

"Crybaby."

"Scaredycat."

The sun had been blazing bright for the last hour. Mark was appreciating the light and heat more than usual when suddenly, a dark cloud passed overhead, blocking the fiery rays. Mark glanced up to see massive clouds moving in. He'd seen storm clouds gather hundreds of times and had never taken much notice of them before. But something felt strange about them this time.

"Those clouds look weird to you?" Mark asked. "Different than normal?"

"No," Dave said, his jaw clenched.

"You didn't even look up."

"I didn't have to. They're perfectly normal."

"Okay, now you're spooking me," Mark told him. "You okay?"

"I'm fine," he growled. "I just have a really pressing desire not to admit I've been watching them coming for the last couple of minutes."

"Worried we'll get some bad weather before we get home?"

"No. I'm worried about what it means that all of those clouds are being blown from different directions so they all converge on the same spot—right on top of us. There's nothing normal about that."

Mark quickly glanced back up. After a few seconds, he realized Dave was right. Clouds usually formed in one spot and then moved in one direction with the wind. Everything should be moving one way, but these clouds appeared to be springing up at the edges of the horizon in all four directions and racing their way toward a fateful meeting in the sky.

"What does it mean? Some kind of crazy storm I've never heard of before?"

"I don't know," Dave snapped. "I'm busy not worrying about it, remember?"

"You'd tell me if--"

Dave suddenly cut the engine. He was muttering under his breath again. Mark wondered if it was Latin.

"What is it?" Mark asked sharply.

"The navigational equipment is going haywire. I don't want to take a chance of us going the wrong direction and getting lost."

Dave tapped one of the gauges. "Come on, work already."

It was growing darker by the moment and Mark looked up again, surveying the strange clouds as everything seemed to grow darker around them. "How far are we from land?"

"My best guess? About an hour and a half."

"You know the heading, right?"

"Yes."

"Then what are we waiting for? Let's get out of here."

"Without instruments--" Dave started.

"We can handle it. Just like the old sailors."

"I told you, that's not all its cracked up to be."

"Don't worry. We still have indoor plumbing. I think you'll be fine," Mark said.

Dave muttered to himself again, definitely in Latin this time, but he throttled the boat up. As soon as he had the boat in gear, he called the Coast Guard and gave them an update on their status. When he mentioned that their instruments weren't working Mark heard the man on the other end tell him to use extreme caution. There was something ominous sounding in the other's voice that he didn't like. Did the Coast Guard know something they didn't?

After Dave ended the call, Mark moved closer. "What exactly are the instruments doing?" he asked, after watching Dave tap one of the gauges a couple more times.

"See for yourself," Dave said.

Mark edged forward until he could see the compass in the center consul. It was spinning round and round like a clock stuck on fast forward. The hair on the back of his neck stood on end.

"What the hell?" he asked.

"My thoughts exactly. I've never prayed a blessing over a ship's control panel before, but now might be an exception."

"No kidding. North can't be in all directions at once."

"And those clouds can't be pushed in from all different directions either, but it's happening."

"What do you think it means?" Mark asked with a sinking feeling in the pit of his stomach.

"I think it means we're in trouble."

"Oh good. I feel much better now. Thanks."

"Mark, am I hallucinating, or do you see that, too?" Dave asked, his voice strained. He pointed ahead of the ship.

Mark glanced in front of him and his stomach turned. Ahead of them, the sea was gray. Farther along, it disappeared altogether in a cloud of white.

"There's fog coming in," he whispered.

6

Sally had just put the first lasagna in the refrigerator and the second into the freezer. She had at least an hour or so before it would be time to put the first one in the oven. She was just finishing up the dishes when her phone rang.

It was Mark.

"Back already?" she cheerfully asked as she picked it up.

There was a lot of static, and then finally she heard his voice. "No. Going to...late. Fog...instruments."

"I can barely hear you. There's interference," she said, raising her voice to match the static. She glanced at her phone to make sure the signal was strong. She had full bars.

There was a particularly strong burst of static and she momentarily pulled the phone away from her ear. Then she heard, "Fog. Late tonight. Tomorrow."

Then the call dropped.

She quickly tried to call back, but it went straight to voicemail. She dropped the phone on the counter and growled in frustration. She'd been so looking forward to this evening.

Oh, well. A delay wasn't the end of the world. The fog would pass, and they'd make it home sooner or later. There went the chance for a quiet, romantic dinner, though. She thought of the negligee in the other room and picked the phone back up.

Hurry home. I have a surprise for you.

She sent the text and felt very pleased with herself, thinking of Mark's expression as he read the text. As she was putting the phone down, her hand froze. A sick feeling washed over her. Her heart began to race and an unreasoning fear suddenly gripped her.

What if he never comes home?

She tried to shake herself, get the feedback loop in her mind to stop.

It's okay. He'll be here before you know it.

~

By the time he hung up with Sally, Mark was beyond frustrated. He wished they'd had a better connection. At least he felt like he'd gotten the message across. He hoped so, anyway. There had been a lot of static.

"How's it going?" he asked Dave as he climbed back up to the wheelhouse.

"The Coast Guard said to sit tight and wait for the sun to start to set so we can get our bearings. They think it will burn through the fog so we'll be able to see it."

"I hope they're right."

"Yeah, me, too. As long as I'm not driving for the next little while, I'd like to have more painkillers, please."

"Sure," Mark said, hurrying down to the cabin to get the bottle. It took him a moment to find it, but once he had he hurried back.

Dave gulped down the pill that Mark gave him.

"You don't look so good," he remarked, more than a little worried.

The priest was pale and sweat beaded his forehead.

"I don't feel so good."

"Maybe you should lie down for a little while."

"Frankly, with my foot hurting as bad as it is, I don't want to try to get back down the ladder or the stairs."

"There's enough room for you to just lie down up here."

"I really don't want to move. I'm not sure if I get out of this chair, whether or not I'll be able to get back into it."

"Well, I've seen you sleep in classes before while sitting upright, so I'm sure you can do it now."

"That was high school."

"And it was hilarious."

"I wish others had been as appreciative."

"Mrs. Foster never even knew."

"Yeah, but Mr. Garcia nearly failed me for it."

Mark was at a loss. He didn't honestly know how to help Dave. He didn't know if he stopped talking if his friend would be able to get some sleep or if the pain would just keep him awake. If it did then talking to him was the better option, maybe it would distract him from the pain.

And the fear. Because of his injury, I'm sure he's feeling it worse than I am right now. If the gauges were working, we'd already be back on the shore where he could get treated in the E.R.

"Can you sleep?" Mark finally asked bluntly.

"I don't know, but I should try."

"Okay. I'll be nearby in case your balance isn't as good as it was in high school."

"Thanks, man."

"Anytime."

Mark climbed down the ladder and took a seat on the main deck where he could keep an eye on Dave. He wanted to try calling Sally back, but he was worried they'd lose power again and he wouldn't be able to recharge his phone. He decided to save the battery in case something like that happened. Part of him argued that he should just take the phone down and plug it in now, but somehow, his phone felt like a lifeline as he held it in his hand. It was connection to home, to Sally and the girls. It hit him that he must be more anxious than he'd realized, since the thought of letting go of his phone, even to charge it, caused him to panic.

So not good. Just pull it together.

~

The hours passed slowly. He dozed off twice himself. Finally, the fog started to lift--not all the way, but just enough

40

that he could see the sun, which was starting to set. He climbed back up the ladder to the wheelhouse. Dave was still in the chair, his head lolled to one side, snoring softly. He hated to wake him, but the sooner they made it home, the sooner Dave could get to a hospital. They couldn't risk losing the light.

"Dave, wake up," he said, shaking his shoulder gently.

Dave blinked several times and then looked up at him. His eyes were glassy and his pupils dilated.

"You okay to drive?" Mark asked anxiously.

Dave nodded slowly, his eyes drifting upward. "Follow the sun."

"Okay. I'm going to stand right here and watch. Then, if you need me to take over, I can."

"Cool."

A minute later, after notifying the Coast Guard that the fog had lifted enough to sail, they were underway. Mark felt his spirits lifting.

Everything was going to be okay. They were headed due west.

~

An hour later, Mark was starting to worry again. Something still wasn't right. "Shouldn't we be seeing land by now?" he asked.

"Yes," Dave said, his jaw clenched and his expression pained. "I've been angling slightly north, just a bit. At this point I don't care where we hit in Florida. We just need to find land."

"Do you want me to radio in?"

Dave nodded, keeping his eyes fixed on the horizon where the sun was slowly sinking.

Mark grabbed the radio. It was already set to Channel 16. He tried raising the Coast Guard. Only static came back over the radio.

Dave swore under his breath, not even bothering with the Latin this time.

41

"I'm with you, buddy."

"We've only got about 15 minutes of sun left. If we haven't found land by then, we're going to have to wait until its completely dark."

"Then what?"

"Hope that we see lights on the coast. Otherwise, we'll send up some flares. We should be close enough that someone is bound to see us."

"You do realize that if fishermen rescue us from the sea, you're never going to live it down at work, right?" Mark asked, weakly attempting to find humor in the situation.

"Yeah. But right now, what I wouldn't give to find some fishers of men."

They lapsed into silence and Mark scanned the horizon anxiously as the sun began to slip beneath the waves. At last it was gone completely. With a weary sigh, Dave slowed the boat and then brought it to a stop.

"And now, we wait," Dave said grimly.

"I know the point of these fishing trips is to relax and do as close to nothing as possible, but I'm getting really tired of just sitting and waiting and doing nothing."

"You could always fish."

Mark stared at Dave, but couldn't tell whether he was trying to be funny or not. Mostly his friend just looked tired and his forehead was furrowed in pain.

"You need some more medication," Mark said.

"Save it. I want to be alert right now."

"How bad is the pain?"

"Don't ask."

"So, read any good books lately?"

Dave turned and looked at him as if he was out of his mind. "Besides the *actual* Good Book?"

Again, they fell silent for a few minutes. Mark kept his eyes fixed on the horizon, hoping to see lights appear. Dave kept looking around, as if he couldn't keep his head still.

"You really think we'll see the lights of the coast?" Mark

finally asked as the sky grew darker.

"Not if the fog reaches us," Dave said softly.

Mark felt a chill dance up his spine as he turned around and realized the fog they had left behind was now swirling toward them across the water, its wispy tentacles reaching out, ready to engulf the boat once again.

"You have got to be kidding me."

~

Sally fell asleep clutching her phone, desperately hoping to hear more from Mark. She'd tried calling a half a dozen times before going to bed, but none of the calls had connected. She felt a sick knot in her gut as she settled down on the bed. She buried her face in his pillow, breathing in the scent of him and missing him desperately.

He's been out on the water hundreds of times. He always comes back. Dave's an expert pilot. They're going to be just fine.

She recited the mantra over and over, hoping it would bring her comfort. Somehow, though, it just made her more agitated with each reiteration until she finally stopped altogether.

After what felt like forever, she drifted to sleep. She was sinking deeper and deeper. She heard Mark's voice and she struggled to answer, but she was falling and couldn't respond.

~

She was on a tiny raft, adrift in a sea of fog. The raft bobbed up and down in the water, which was dark and choppy. Waves splashed over the edges and she desperately tried to edge away from the water. Something terrible was lurking beneath her. She knew it, but she was too afraid to glance over the side and see for herself exactly what was there. All she knew was that it was circling her, coming closer and closer. It bumped the underside of her raft and she screamed as the one side of the raft lifted

43

into the air, only to drop back down with a crash.

It's going to get me.

It's going to consume me.

There was nothing she could do. There was no one around. She could shout for help forever and no one would ever hear her.

Whatever it was slammed into the bottom of the raft again, raising it up out of the water entirely. Then the whole raft crashed down and nearly capsized. She clung to the logs of the raft, digging her fingernails into the cracks, clawing and trying to hold on.

She had to look. She had to know what was stalking her, what was trying to kill her.

In the distance she heard Mark's voice. He was calling her. He needed her. She crawled over to the edge of the raft and gazed down into the darkness below. Then she began to scream.

7

Mark woke up with a shout, sweat dotting his brow. He'd fallen asleep in one of the chairs on deck and had a nightmare that Sally was trapped on a raft in the middle of the ocean with a monster from the depths trying to kill her. He'd shouted and shouted, trying to warn her, but it hadn't helped.

"What's wrong?" Dave asked sharply.

"Sorry. Bad dream. I fell asleep."

"Unfortunately, you don't have to fall asleep to have a bad dream."

"What does that mean?" Mark asked.

"There's something wrong with the ocean." Dave's voice was tight.

Mark hastily stood up. "What do you mean *wrong*?"

"Last night, I thought it must be my imagination. I haven't gotten much sleep lately. I've been working too hard."

Dave's voice had an eeriness to it that made Mark's hair stand on end.

"You're sleep deprived now. And you're in a lot of pain."

"You think it's just my imagination? Go ahead. I dare you. Look at the ocean."

Mark hesitated. "I don't want to."

Maybe if he didn't look at it, it would go away.

"Look!"

Mark walked to the side of the boat. He didn't know why, but he was shaking. Hesitantly, he glanced down. The boat's running lights were on, but the fog muted them a mere foot away from the boat.

No! It wasn't fog.

Darkness.

45

He shuddered.

He looked up at the sky. Just as it had been the previous night, there was no moon. Everything was pitch black. There were no stars, either.

"We're lost," he said, the words escaping his lips before he even knew he was going to utter them.

"Yes."

"I've spent a lot of my life on the water. So have you. Have you ever seen this…this…*darkness* before? Or anything even remotely like it?"

"Not until last night," Dave said. "I should have realized then that we were in trouble."

"You're really freaking me out now."

"Imagine how I feel."

Mark moved over to the ladder. He didn't know what he was going to do when he got to the top, but giving Dave a hard shake was at the top of his list. He was halfway up when something slammed into the boat.

He lost his grip and fell, landing with a thud on his back and knocking the breath from his lungs. He realized with a gasp that the ship was starting to tilt violently.

"We're going to capsize!" Dave shouted.

The whole world was spinning. A wave came from out of nowhere and crashed over the top of them. Mark sucked in seawater and his lungs burned like they were on fire. He tried to cough, but more water kept slamming down on him, filling nose and mouth.

I can't breathe!

The boat tilted harder. He could hear things slamming about down below.

We're going over!

Another wave crested over the boat and came crashing down on top of him. He couldn't see and he couldn't breathe. His ears filled with a roaring sound. He had no idea where Dave was. The water stopped and he desperately gasped for a breath of air, twisting on his side as he coughed up water.

46

"Dave!" he screamed, his voice hoarse from the seawater. He hoped the other man hadn't been swept overboard.

"Hold on!" Dave yelled back.

The boat spun right before another wave hit it hard. He could hear Dave on the radio.

"Mayday, mayday. This is the vessel *The Guardians*. We are caught in some sort of freak storm. Waves are threatening to capsize us. We can't hold out much longer. We have no idea where we are. We believe we should be close to Miami, but our navigation is out. Two men on board, one badly injured. Need help. Mayday. Can anyone hear me?"

Mark struggled to his hands and knees, only to be knocked flat on his back a moment later when another wave slammed into the ship.

"Do something!" he shouted.

"I'm trying!"

The boat lurched forward, only to be spun around again. Through it all Mark was aware of one thing, which to him was more horrific than everything else he could conjure. The darkness that had been pressing in had made its way onto the ship itself. He could barely see Dave struggling with the wheel. It was as if the darkness was swallowing up first him, and then the ship.

"Dave!"

His voice was swallowed up just as it had been the night before, only worse. He shouted at the top of his lungs, his throat burning and aching, but he could only hear the faintest whisper. Panic seized him. He was with his best friend and yet he was going to die alone. Unheard. Unseen.

The boat spun again. Mark was completely turned around. He had no idea which direction the bow was facing, and with the darkness all around him, he couldn't see anything. He crawled blindly across the deck, the dark and the noise serving to completely confuse his senses. He closed his eyes and struggled just to focus on the feeling of the deck beneath his hands. It was wet and his hands were stinging as though salt

47

water was hitting cuts he wasn't aware he had. He grit his teeth against the pain and kept reaching out, trying to feel something--a chair, a table--anything that might help him get his bearings.

His hand finally struck something solid. It felt like a wall. He didn't know if he had made it to the bow or the wall on which the wheelhouse was perched. He moved slowly, feeling his way as best he could, not wanting to accidentally tumble head first down the stairs to the deck below.

He struggled to his knees moments before the ship lurched again, shuddering in the opposite direction of where it had been moving.

It threw him back down but he managed to keep a hand on the wall. He was screaming and screaming but he couldn't hear himself. The waves of water and sound and darkness crashed over him again and again.

He reached his left hand up as high as he could and finally felt one of the anchors which kept the fishing rods in place.

He was at the stern. Resolutely, he turned. It took all of his courage, but he let go of the wall and started slipping and sliding and crawling his way back across the deck, trying to reach the other side.

He had no idea what had happened to Dave, whether he was still in the captain's chair or had been swept overboard. In the absolute darkness, there was no chance of climbing up the ladder and taking the wheel, especially since he'd be steering completely blind.

I have to get below deck.

If the boat finally flipped, it would be the worst place he could be, but one more good roll and he might find himself in the water.

Alone, blind and without any kind of life preserver, he wouldn't survive more than a minute in this storm. So far, the ship had stayed afloat, and he had to hope it would continue to do so.

He was frightened and exhausted. He knew he couldn't give up, though, because he had three of the most precious treasures in the world waiting for him at home.

He had to make it back.

He couldn't leave Sally and the girls alone. It was unthinkable.

Tears of frustration rolled down his cheeks, mingling with the saltwater that was already there. Through his mind, a montage of images started playing, like some perverse movie made to torture him. It wasn't his life flashing in front of his eyes, because he wasn't seeing his past. He was seeing his family's future without him.

He pictured Sally grieving at his funeral, with Emma and little Jayne clinging to her and sobbing. Jayne was too young to really understand, but she was crying because her mother and sister were. She wanted her daddy but had been told he was in a better place and he wasn't coming back.

How could any place where he was there and they weren't be better? he wondered bitterly.

He saw Emma and Jayne growing up without a father. He watched how hard it was on Sally to try to be both mother and father to them and how she struggled every day with burdens she shouldn't have had to bear. He saw his daughters graduate from high school and then college without him there to cheer them on. Strangers walked both of them down the aisle at their weddings.

He couldn't let that happen.

He would die for his family if it came to that, but right now he needed to live for them.

Live, no matter what it took, no matter how impossible.

Sally, Emma, Jayne.

With each move he made, he chanted their names, letting them be the force driving him forward. He could do this for them. He could beat this storm—and whatever other unknown evils he was facing--for them.

He couldn't judge how far he had gone, but he was sure he had to be getting close to the wall with the stairwell.

What if it was already completely flooded down below?

He should have thought about that, he realized. It must certainly be underwater by now. His hand struck the wall painfully and he sucked in a breath. He hesitated, wondering where he could possibly hide to try and weather out whatever was happening.

Without warning, something heavy fell on top of him with a thud. Instinctively, he jerked, pushing and kicking at whatever it was until he connected with something soft.

A hand reached out and grabbed his shoulder.

Dave. It's Dave, he told himself, struggling to calm down.

His friend pulled him closer. He still couldn't see him, but he grabbed Dave's shoulder as well, not wanting to get separated in the whirlwind.

Finally, he felt Dave's head touch his. His friend was leaning toward his ear, struggling to tell him something. Dave's hands were gripping onto him like bands of steel. Mark tilted his head, trying to listen. Then he heard the faintest whisper of sound, which he instinctively knew was Dave shouting as loud as he could.

"We're in trouble."

~

Sally awoke just after seven. She hadn't slept well thanks to the nightmare, so she rose early and started making breakfast, She felt far too anxious to try to sleep anymore.

Something was wrong. She could feel it. She'd tried calling Mark but it went straight to voicemail without even ringing. That wasn't right. She bit her bottom lip as her stomach twisted itself into knots.

She turned back to the counter, steadied herself for a moment, and then grabbed an egg out of the carton.

Suddenly the doorbell rang, startling her. She dropped the egg. It cracked and broke open when it hit the ground, oozing all over the floor. She stepped over it and headed to the front door.

They never had visitors this early. Her mind raced ahead, trying to imagine who was waiting on the other side of the door. Perhaps it was Mark and he had forgotten his key. She reached it and hastily threw it open.

Standing on the porch were two police officers. They both looked at her grimly. Her heart stopped for a moment as she realized the significance of their presence at her home.

"Sally White?" the taller one asked.

"No," she whispered raggedly, realizing Mark was gone.

8

"Ma'am, I'm Officer Fordham and this is Officer Ramirez," the taller of the two uniformed men said. "May we come in?"

"My husband. What's happened to him?" she gasped, her voice cracking.

"Ma'am, perhaps it would be better if we could speak inside," Ramirez suggested.

"Tell me now," she begged.

"Ma'am, we plan on doing that. We'd like you to sit down first," Fordham said.

She turned and walked over to the couch in the living room, clenching her hands together until her fingernails dug into the skin. She tried to sit down, but her legs betrayed her and she collapsed into the chair.

The officers came inside, closing the door behind them. They moved over near her and took seats.

Officer Fordham took a deep breath. "Ma'am, at approximately 2:30 yesterday afternoon, the Coast Guard lost contact with your husband's boat. At 10:30 p.m., they received a garbled distress call indicating that one of the men was injured and they were being battered by a storm with heavy waves. Attempts to establish two-way communication failed."

"What does that mean?" she croaked, trying to comprehend what he was saying.

Injured. Storm. Failed communication...

Officer Ramirez cleared his throat. "It means that while the Coast Guard was able to receive part of their distress call they were unable to confirm that the captain heard their response. They sent ships out looking for your husband's boat immediately afterward to the last known coordinates, but they have yet to find anything."

"Anyone, you mean. Just tell me straight. Is he dead?" She forced herself to actually say the word, but then had to swallow back the bile that burned the back of her throat.

The two men exchanged a glance. "They don't know anything for certain at this point," Fordham finally said. "As soon as the sun rose, they sent out more ships and a couple of helicopters. Given how close they were to shore when they lost their instruments, there is good reason to believe they will soon be found."

"Even though they were being hit by a storm with heavy waves? Couldn't that have thrown them farther out to sea?"

"There is always reason to hope and pray," Ramirez said, not directly answering her question. "Please rest assured that the Coast Guard is doing everything within their power to locate them and bring them home safely to you."

"What do the odds look like right now?"

The two officers glanced at each other. "Frankly, it's hard to say," Fordham said slowly. "A lot of factors go into something like this."

"But the Coast Guard is searching?"

"Yes, ma'am."

Abruptly, she stood up and went to grab her purse. The two officers stood and trailed after her.

"Ma'am, what are you doing?"

"I'm going down to talk to the Coast Guard. There's nothing more you guys can tell me. I need to be where I can hear what's happening, where I can help."

"There's nothing you can--"

She spun around. "Don't tell me what I can and can't do! I know Mark and Dave better than anyone. I know how they think and what they'd do. Don't you tell me I can't be useful and that there's nothing I can do. Even if that's true, I choose to do nothing there instead of here by myself."

She was screaming at the men. She knew it wasn't their fault, but she couldn't seem to stop herself. Both men backed off slowly.

"Ma'am, you really shouldn't drive in the state you're in," Fordham said softly, clearly trying to be gentle with her.

He was right.

She knew he was right.

At the moment, she couldn't even remember how to get to the marina, let alone the Coast Guard station.

"Thank you. I accept your offer to drive me," she said.

The police officers appeared taken aback. Ramirez looked as if he was about to protest when she pinned him with her gaze. "Unless you really want me on the road right now," she said pointedly.

"We'd be happy to drop you off and let you speak with someone," Fordham said hastily.

"Great. Let's go."

A minute later, she was in the back seat of their squad car. With shaking fingers, she pulled up her mom's name on her phone. She called and pressed the phone to her cheek.

"Hi, dear. Are you about ready to pick up the girls?" her mother asked.

"No. I'm sorry, Mom. I--I need you to keep them a little longer."

"Is there something wrong? You don't sound good."

"Please don't tell the girls, but Mark's boat went missing. The Coast Guard are searching for it now."

Her mom gasped on the other end of the line. "Oh, no!"

"I'm going down to the Coast Guard station to find out more and see if I can be of any assistance to them."

"What can we do to help?"

"Just tell Emma and Jayne Mama and Daddy love them and we'll see them soon," she said, struggling to get the words out around the lump in her throat.

"Okay. If you need anything, you call. And please try to keep in touch to let us know how it's going, even if it's just a quick text message."

"I will, Mama. I promise," Sally said before hanging up.

54

She couldn't do anything to stave off the torrent of tears that suddenly flooded her eyes and poured down her cheeks. She tried her best to keep them in, but she couldn't. She felt sick-- hot and cold all over, as if she had the stomach flu with a high fever. Around her, it was as if things were moving in slow motion, like a dream.

She stared out the window of the police cruiser at the world going by. She could see happy people, busy going about their day, completely oblivious to the fact that the world was coming to an end.

How did they not know? She wanted to scream at them that the greatest man in the world was missing, that he might even be dead. She wanted to stop them in their tracks and wipe the grins off their faces as she told them the horror of what was happening. How dare they be happy when everything was crashing down around her?

She let out a broken sob, no longer caring if the men in the front of the car could hear her crying. The whole world *should* be crying with her. She leaned her head against the window and closed her eyes as tightly as she could. She tried to wish it all away, but she could still feel the car as it twisted and turned through the streets. She could hear the squawk of the police radio. She could feel her heart ripping into tiny shreds. All of it meant this was real. It was all happening, whether she chose to believe it or not.

Her tears flowed faster, streaming down her face in hot rivulets to drip off her chin and onto her shirt. She no longer cared. This much pain couldn't be contained. It was as if every horrible thing that had ever happened taken all together couldn't possibly compare to the pain and despair of this one moment.

I can't live without him.

I won't live without him.

The words kept rattling round and round in her head. And over and through it all, she kept hearing high-pitched screaming. It was as if part of her mind was just screaming without end, unable to cope with the horror presented to it.

55

"It's early yet. They may still find him."

"What?" she asked, struggling to understand what Fordham was saying.

"It's amazing what they can do these days to find ships that have gone missing. If he's out there, they'll find him," he said with more assurance in his tone.

"Thank you," she said, tasting the salt of her tears on her lips.

With everything she had in her, she wanted to believe him. She wanted it so bad that it scared her.

It hasn't been that long. There's still time.

She felt as if her mind was shattering, splitting in two. There was the part that refused to believe he was gone and the part that had already lost hope and had surrendered to her grief. They were battling against each other, making her head pound uncontrollably.

Suddenly the car came to a stop.

"We're here," Ramirez said.

"Here?"

"The Coast Guard station," Fordham said. "Do you want me to escort you inside, find someone with whom you can speak?"

"Yes, please," she said, feeling her throat go dry and her legs go numb. He was being so nice to her, and she had yelled at him.

The part of her that had already given up wanted nothing more than to crawl into a dark corner somewhere and be left alone to cry and lick her wounds. The other part of her was determined to bring him back through the sheer force of her love for him.

Officer Fordham opened the door for her and she stepped out, her legs shaky. She held onto the door for a moment to regain her balance and then let go of it in favor of the arm he extended to her. She grabbed onto it as if it were a life preserver and she was drowning.

Did Mark drown?

Is he alive, but clinging to a life preserver in the middle of the ocean?

Is Dave with him?

So many questions raced through her mind. They'd said one of the men had been injured. Was it Mark or Dave?

She wished she knew something, anything. She was still crying so hard that she couldn't even really see where she was going. She just held on to Officer Fordham's arm and let him steer her wherever he was leading her.

"Captain, this is Mrs. White" she heard him say after they came to a stop.

She looked up and saw a man staring at her. He was a couple of years older than her with a suntanned face and solemn eyes.

"You can call me John," he told her.

"I'm Sally," she managed to get out.

"Thank you, officer. I'll take it from here," John murmured.

Fordham gently extricated himself from her grip. She felt unsteady on her feet and John quickly led her to a chair a few steps away.

"Please. Sit down before you fall down," he instructed.

There was something in his tone which conveyed that he was a man who stood for no nonsense, and for some reason, that reassured her. She immediately sat as he asked.

She attempted to dash away her tears and he handed her a box of tissues. She took it gratefully and wiped her eyes and cheeks before finally blowing her nose. She wadded up the tissues in her fist and held onto them tightly. She blinked through the tears, trying to focus enough to see where there might be a trash can.

Instead, the first thing she noticed when her vision cleared was a giant status board with the name of her husband's ship on it. Her stomach lurched suddenly, and she pointed anxiously at the board.

"That's my husband's ship," she said, her voice hoarse. "They were just going fishing. Just fishing," she repeated lamely.

57

John nodded grimly. "I want to assure you we are doing everything we can to find it, along with your husband and his captain."

"Dave. He's a priest. They've been friends since elementary school. He used to be in the navy."

"Hopefully everything he learned will serve him out there today."

"I don't understand. How did this happen?" she asked.

"We don't exactly understand either," John admitted, taking a seat beside her. "They radioed in reporting some anomalous conditions which frankly, no other ships or radar systems have verified."

"What anomalous conditions?" she asked.

"The biggest problem, as I understand it from their somewhat-garbled transmissions, was intense, white-out foggy conditions."

"Fog can happen," she said, struggling to understand what was unusual about this. "And boats have special navigation systems to get them through bad weather, right?"

"Yes, ma'am, but they're the only ones who reported seeing it in the whole area. That leads us to believe that either they weren't where they thought they were or…"

"Or what?"

"Or they were in some way impaired, maybe from excessive drinking or perhaps drug use?" he suggested, eyeing her closely.

She shook her head fiercely. "No. No way. I can tell you right now that isn't the case, not with either of them. It can't be that."

"That doesn't really leave us with many other possibilities."

"Well, there has to be another answer. Dave is a great captain and they're both experienced fishermen. They've been out there dozens of times. They know the ocean. They know the waters and the course."

"Normally I'd be inclined to agree with you," he said.

"Normally?" she said, latching onto the word. The muscles

58

in her shoulders tightened. Did he not believe her? Did he think Mark and Dave were out there drunk, or stoned, or worse?

"Like I said, there have been no other reports of adverse conditions. We know for a fact that several ships passed near their reported locations several times over the past thirty-six hours, and yet none of them made any sighting of your husband's boat."

"How is that possible?"

"That's why we're investigating the theory that they weren't where they said they were."

"They wouldn't give you a false location on purpose, especially not if they were calling for help," she said. "If one of them was hurt, they'd want you to be able to find them. It just doesn't make sense."

"It wouldn't make a lot of sense no, unless they had an even better reason to hide their location."

"What are you saying?" she snapped, her nerves frayed and her frustration mounting. "Are you accusing them of what--of being smugglers? No way. Why don't you stop assuming they did something wrong and start looking for them!"

"Ma'am, we are looking for them," he said, taking a deep breath. "It's also possible that they thought they were exactly where they said they were, but they were confused or misled by instruments which had somehow ceased working."

The screaming in her head grew louder. Mark and Dave were out there somewhere in trouble, and this guy just wanted to talk around and around the problem. She pressed her shaking hands to her head.

"Look, I know this is hard," John said. "And believe me, we are doing everything we can to find them. It would be best if you just go home and get some rest."

"I am not leaving here without my husband!" she shouted at him.

"Okay, just calm down." He held up his hands palms out, as if in surrender. "I don't want to have to call Officer Fordham to come back and pick you up."

59

"Okay," she said, struggling to get a grip on her emotions, which were flailing wildly inside her.

I'm like a drowning animal, she thought.

The image brought to mind so many others. She couldn't think of Mark or Dave going through that. She forced herself to take several slow, deep breaths.

"That's better," John said, his voice soothing. "Now, did you have any contact with them after they left?"

She nodded slowly. "We talked on Saturday. We mostly texted. I kept getting a lot of weird static when we tried to actually speak on the phone. It's never been that bad when they've gone out fishing in the past."

"Can you remember anything else strange about your exchanges?" he asked.

She struggled to think through the dense fog that was wrapping around her mind.

It's just like the fog that wrapped around the boat.

"Um, yes. The text messages were taking a really long time to go back and forth."

"How long?" John asked sharply, leaning forward.

She shook her head. "Long, like a minute or more. Here. You can see the timestamps," she said. She pulled up the conversation and handed her phone to John. He scrolled through it, his brow furrowed in concentration.

"Odd," he muttered under his breath.

"Does it mean anything? Does it help?"

"I don't know. It may mean something. But anything else you can remember, please share it."

"Anything. Everything. I just want him back."

"We want that, as well."

A younger man walked into the room, studying a paper in his hand. "Captain, we've got three birds up and we've put out the word to all vessels in the area to keep a look out for the boat. If it's still in our ocean, we'll--" He glanced up from the paper and abruptly stopped talking.

"This is Mrs. White," John said pointedly.

60

"Sorry, I'll come back later," the man said hastily.

"No, please! Are you talking about my husband?"

He glanced at John, who nodded.

"Yes, ma'am."

"What did you mean when you said st*ill in our ocean*? Where else would they be?"

The young man became more flustered than he already was and dropped his eyes. "It's just a saying, ma'am. If the ship is still floating and hasn't sank… er, I mean, we'll find it," he said, struggling to finish his sentence.

"Thank you. That will be all," John said, his voice tight.

The fog seemed to be lifting from her brain. Now, instead, it felt as if everything was in super sharp focus. John was clearly displeased with the younger man, and she felt it wasn't just because he'd said the word *sank* in front of her. There was something else.

"What was that about?" she asked in a no-nonsense tone.

"Nothing. Guys aren't used to talking in front of civilians," he said briefly in response.

His voice sounded calm, but she noticed he wouldn't meet her eyes.

"Look me in the eyes when you tell me that."

He jerked as though stung. He glanced up at her and looked slightly unsettled.

"It wasn't *nothing*," she growled, clenching her fists. "It wasn't just that he didn't know what to say."

"Ma'am--"

"Don't ma'am me. At least have the decency to use my name if you're going to lie to me."

"I am not lying to you."

She took a deep breath. "John, please. Just tell me the truth. What are you hiding from me?"

Her phone chimed. They both looked at it. John still had a hold of it and his eyes widened.

He handed it to her. "It looks like someone left you a message," he said, his tone gruff.

"Who?" she asked, grabbing the phone from him. "Your husband."

9

"I missed his call!" Sally gasped. "He's alive!" She clutched the phone and played the voicemail.

"Hey, babe, it's me. I miss you. I love you. Goodbye."

She pulled the phone away from her ear and stared at it as tears filled her eyes.

"What is it? What did he say?" John asked.

She put it on speaker as she replayed the message.

"Hey, babe, it's me. I miss you. I love you. Goodbye."

He looked up at her. "He sounds remarkably… calm."

She bit her lip. "I…I don't know what this means."

"He said in the texts he sent you Saturday night that he'd tried calling but ended up leaving you a voicemail that you said never showed up. Could this be it?"

She sagged in her chair, feeling all of the fight go out of her. "Yes, that makes sense." Tears welled in her eyes again. "What if that's the last time I ever hear his voice?" she asked raggedly.

"You can't think that way. We're still out there looking for him. You have to keep hoping and be strong for him."

"What's the longest someone's ever been missing and then been found alive?" she asked.

"A long time," John said soothingly. "They should have plenty of water on board."

"I know they have fish," she said.

He chuckled. "Yeah, they'll never want to eat fish again once they get back."

"My freezer would be grateful," she said, forcing a dry chuckle. "Do you really believe there's actually a chance that they're okay?"

"I do."

"The officers said something about one of them being injured."

"From what we can tell, we think it was the pilot."

"Dave," she said, feeling a surge of relief and then immediately feeling guilty. "Is it bad that I'm glad it's him and not Mark?"

"No. Under the circumstances, that's a perfectly understandable reaction."

"Oh, good."

"Would you like some coffee?"

Sally nodded. Her emotions were out of control and skidding all over the place. Maybe some coffee would help calm her nerves and let her think.

John got up and left the room. She looked around and realized it was his office. It was lined with pictures of different ships, some quite old looking and others much more modern. It seemed like a pretty random hodgepodge and she couldn't help but wonder if there was any sort of rhyme or reason to which pictures were included on the walls. The picture closest to her was a drawing of an old-looking sailing ship. She could just make out the name *USS Wasp* underneath the drawing. Then her eyes fell on a photograph of what looked like a tanker. She squinted her eyes and could just make out the words *SS Marine Sulphur Queen*.

Another picture was a modern one. It showed two boys standing in front of a fishing boat, both grinning from ear-to-ear. The boat was probably about 19-feet long, less than half the size of *The Guardians*.

"Here you go," John said, returning with the coffee.

She took it, wrapping her hands around it. The heat felt good. She brought it slowly to her lips, breathing in the rich aroma. She finally took a swallow and it warmed her insides.

"What is the average length of time someone is missing before they're found?" she asked.

He shook his head. "I don't know. Every case is different and it takes as long as it takes. Given the size of your husband's boat, it should be easier to spot than some others we've found. So, theoretically that could cut down on the search time considerably."

"But it might not."

"Like I said, we're still trying to figure out why *The Guardians* was reporting adverse weather conditions when no one else in the area they were supposedly in had anything amiss on their radars."

"Couldn't fog and other weather be isolated in small areas? I mean, I have a cousin who lives in San Francisco and she's always talking about driving in and out of patches of fog. Oh, and then there's those rainstorms where you can actually see the line where the rain stops. Sometimes it's raining on one side of the street and not the other."

"While all that is true, it's just unusual that there would be a fog bank as pervasive and long-lasting as what they were describing for where they were. Usually, fog burns off, but apparently it lasted most of the day yesterday. You would think that somebody else would have noticed something like that."

"What if Dave wasn't thinking straight because he was injured and he sailed farther out to sea instead of back toward Miami?"

"We thought about that. We're also accounting for him possibly drifting north or south. We've reached out to other stations to help with the search and ones farther out just to keep an eye out."

She nodded. The coffee was helping to clear her head, but a sense of helplessness was settling in just as fast. The police officers had been right. There really was nothing she could do here.

Even so, she refused to go. She wanted to hear whatever they heard when they heard it and not a single second later.

"You feeling a little better?" John asked, sizing her up.

"Yes, thank you. I appreciate the coffee."

"How about if you go home and get some rest and I'll call as soon as I know anything."

"No. I'm not leaving."

"Please, Sally. Let us do our jobs."

"I'll just sit here silently. You don't have to talk to me. I promise I won't get in the way. I just want to be here the second any news comes in."

"Look, the guys are already anxious and on edge without seeing you here. It's putting extra pressure on them."

"Maybe when they get tired of seeing me it will remind them just how important it is that they keep searching until they find my husband."

"Look. They don't *need* a reminder. They know exactly how important it is and they will do everything in their power to find the ship. The last thing we need at the moment is to have you underfoot."

She stared at him steadily. "Just answer me this. Would you leave if they were searching for your wife?"

His shoulders slumped in defeat. "No. No, I wouldn't."

"So, how can you ask me to do what you couldn't?"

"All right. You can stay. But if you cause a fuss, I will have you removed from here. Understand?"

She nodded, struggling to stay focused on the feeling of the warm coffee cup in her hands. One of her college roommates had gone on to be a trauma counselor. She always said that when you were overwhelmed and freaking out, to fixate on tactile feelings, such as the feeling of the warm ceramic mug against her hands.

She wasn't sure if it was working or not. Maybe she was just going into shock or becoming numb. Whatever was happening, she didn't fight it. She couldn't stand another wave of chaos in her mind just then. It was too much.

Just focus on the coffee and on the fact that Mark will come home to us. We'll drink coffee that's much better than this and the whole family will be together.

She settled into her chair, quietly watching as John went in and out of the office. She listened carefully whenever someone spoke with him about the search.

Time passed. He offered her some food, but she wasn't hungry. Her stomach was turning over too much to try to put food in it. She just sat and slowly drank her coffee. Between a horrible night's sleep and the bad news in the morning, she was thoroughly exhausted. At some point she realized the coffee was all that was keeping her awake.

The minutes ticked by with agonizing slowness. Finally, a man walked in and dropped some papers on John's desk. "The birds are refueling sir. They're searching the tertiary quadrant next."

"No sign of anything?" John asked, an edge to his voice.

"Nothing, sir. No boat, no lifeboats and no wreckage."

John visibly winced when the man said *wreckage*, but Sally breathed a sigh of relief. Sometimes no news was good news. In this case, no wreckage definitely counted as good news.

The man left the office and John began to leaf through the papers. She wanted to say something, but she had promised not to get in his way, and, really, she had nothing more to add at that moment.

After more time had passed, she got up to stretch her legs. She glanced at some more of the pictures on the walls before excusing herself to the restroom. She returned a couple of minutes later and resumed her silent vigil.

Sit, drink coffee, think about Mark. Repeat.

Another man came in and reported that the search boats had yet to find anything, either. Apparently, they had people combing through the last communiques with the boat before it disappeared. As dearly as she wanted to hear those, she continued to sit and wait.

After another hour, it seemed as if all her life, all she'd been doing was waiting.

John finally looked up at her. "You okay?"

"Yes."

"Anything I can get you?"

"No."

"Any questions?"

"About the search? No. I've heard everything you've heard."

"Questions about anything else?"

"Actually, I have one question about all these ships on the walls," she said, pointing to the pictures she had been staring at.

"Yes?"

"They're from all different time periods, including that one of the two boys who look like the picture could have been taken yesterday."

"That picture was taken in 2015," he said, without even looking at the picture in question.

"That makes sense. The boys look so happy standing there. Are these the ships this station has saved?"

He shook his head grimly. "No, these were ships we couldn't save. All of them were lost."

The revelation startled her. She kept staring at the one picture, feeling a sick twisting sensation in the pit of her stomach.

"The boys--" she started to ask, but couldn't get the rest of the words out.

"Yes, the boys were lost, too. They were fourteen and went on a fishing trip together. The boat was found a year later. It was in decent shape, but there was no sign of the boys."

As the horror of what he was saying washed over Sally, she felt instant heartbreak for the families of the boys and a renewed sense of urgency to find Mark and Dave. She didn't want a year to go by before *The Guardians* showed up without them.

As a deluge of emotions rushed through her, she struggled to get a grip on them, her eyes zeroed in on a blank section of wall. She saw a flash of something, just for a moment, and then it was gone. It was a picture of a boat she knew well.

She sucked in her breath as she realized that John would soon be putting up a picture of her husband's boat on that spot.

10

The phone rang, startling her so much she nearly dropped her mug. As she jumped, she sloshed some of the coffee on her hand. John answered after the first ring, and moments later he began to scowl. She kept her eyes glued to his face, trying to glean what she could by watching his facial expressions and body language.

He finally hung up the phone and sat still for several seconds, not moving.

"Wh--What is it?" she stammered, her mouth having gone dry.

"A storm's moving in. A big one. We'll have to call off the search until it's over," John said bluntly.

He wouldn't look at her.

It's over.

She knew it.

He picked up a stress ball off his desk, squeezed it a couple of times and then suddenly threw it at the wall. It hit with a loud *thunk*. Even though she saw him throw it, the sound made her jump again.

He stood abruptly, and began to pace, jamming his fingers through his hair.

"Of all the lousy timing," he muttered to himself, voice tinged with anger and regret. "Son-of-a..."

He turned to her then, and she could see her own hopelessness mirrored in his eyes.

"I promise we'll go back out the moment it's safe to do so."

"But you think this is it—the end. If they're not gone now, they will be by the time you get to them," she said, her voice shaking uncontrollably.

"I'm not going to lie to you. The odds of us finding them alive have just dropped considerably. But we're not giving up. *I'm* not giving up."

Her eyes drifted to the blank spot on the wall. "You're going to put the picture of my husband's ship up there, aren't you?" she asked, pointing an accusatory finger at it.

"I pray I don't have to," he said forcefully.

She nodded.

"Look, the storm's set to last at least twelve hours. You need to go home and get some sleep. I'm not asking this time. You'll need it later. No matter what happens."

"I don't want to go home," she admitted.

"I understand. There's a hotel down the block. I'll have one of the guys run you over and you can stay there for a while."

"Thank you," she said, rising unsteadily to her feet. "I'm not giving up hope."

"Neither am I."

"All right. I will see you first thing in the morning."

His lips pressed into a stark line as he nodded to her.

~

An hour later, she had showered and crawled into her hotel bed. She lay on her side of the bed, facing Mark's side. She kept rubbing her hand over the pillow where his head should have been. She had spent what was left of her tears in the shower and now she was too exhausted even to move, other than to curl more deeply into the sheets.

She closed her eyes, trying to picture Mark there beside her. She pretended for just a moment that she could hear his laugh. Her body sunk further into the mattress as her muscles relaxed. She didn't know how long she'd sat in the chair in John's office, but it had felt like an eternity.

An eternity waiting to hear anything.

An eternity waiting to hear that they had found *The Guardians*.

An eternity waiting to hear where her husband was.

Oh, Mark, she thought as she drifted to sleep. *Where are you?*

~

Pain hammered at every inch of his body, jolting him awake. Mark was still for a moment, trying to remember where he was and what had happened to him. Slowly, everything started to come back. The boat. The storm. Dave telling him that they were in some kind of trouble.

He didn't really remember much after that.

He slowly opened his eyes, half-afraid of what he'd see—or what he *wouldn't* see.

Darkness.

It was dark out, but the world was bathed in a silvery glow from the half moon shining high in the sky. He blinked at it, remembering something that Dave had said about how there was supposed to be a full moon right now. But there obviously wasn't.

"Dave?" he croaked, his throat dry and scratchy from the saltwater and his voice unrecognizable even to him. "Dave?" he called louder before falling into a coughing fit.

"Dave's not here right now," he heard his friend say.

"Good, because I need to talk to someone who can actually explain what's happening here."

"That's not me, er, Dave."

"You alive?"

"Apparently," Dave said with a groan.

"Where are we?"

"On the ship. At least, it feels like it."

Well, at least they hadn't gone overboard.

"The storm is over."

"Looks like."

"We should probably try sitting up," Mark said.

"You first. I don't want to—I really, really don't want to"

Mark couldn't say he blamed him. If he was feeling this bad, he couldn't imagine how much pain Dave had to be in with his broken foot.

He rolled over onto his side and from there he gingerly sat up, testing every joint and muscle as he went. He experienced shooting pain all over his body, but it didn't feel as if anything was broken. He was near one of the chairs and managed to stand up just enough so he could slide into it. He was surprised to find that it was already dried out which made him wonder how long they'd been unconscious.

David lay face down on the deck a couple of feet away from him. Every inch of exposed skin was covered with mottled bruises and Mark cringed at the sight. Then he looked at his own arms and realized they looked no better. They'd both been battered and bruised by the storm.

He stared out at the ocean, which now looked calm, tranquil even. There was no hint of the ravaging storm which had tried to kill them only hours earlier. He gazed across the horizon, but there was only ocean as far as the eye could see. He glanced back up at the sky, looking for a constellation he would recognize.

Dave slowly rolled over and sat up, groaning in pain as he did so. "Any idea where we are?"

"Not really. The ocean is visible, and at least the moon is out now. I can see Orion," Mark said, pointing to the constellation.

"That's impossible."

Mark turned to look at Dave. "What are you talking about? It's right there."

All the color drained from Dave's face. "You don't understand. Orion can only be seen in our area in the winter."

Mark frowned. "It's autumn. What does that mean?"

"We're either way, way off course or…"

"Or what?"

"Or we've time-traveled."

"Okay, so how far off course do you think we've gone?"

"I don't know. I can't even begin to guess. I'll have to study the sky and the other constellations to try and figure it out. Of course, it would help if we could see land anywhere," Dave said, the frustration in his voice rising. "It'd be much easier just to go to shore—wherever—so we know for sure where we are. How many flares do we have left?"

"Assuming they survived the storm? Two red and one orange."

"What do you think?"

"I think we should send a red one up now while it's dark enough to show up nice and bright. Anyone out looking for us, or anyone out here at all, for that matter, should be able to see it for miles. Hopefully someone will come to our rescue."

"Okay, let's do it."

Dave struggled to get up but he gritted his teeth and sucked in a breath.

"How about I help you into a chair and then I send up the flare?"

Dave nodded as his face contorted with pain.

~

Mark sent up the flare and then decided to take stock of what supplies they had down below. After a few minutes, he brought up bottled water, packaged food and medication. "Well, the good news is, we won't starve," he said as he presented his findings to Dave. "At least not for a while yet."

"If starvation was an option, I'd tell you to save yourself and shoot me now," Dave said, without a hint of a smile.

"Pain that bad?"

Dave didn't respond as he reached for the painkillers.

~

A half an hour later, after forcing down some food, Dave fell into a restless sleep. Mark knew under the circumstances, rest was the best thing for his friend, so despite being on edge, he didn't wake him. He figured he could keep watch for any ships that might be coming their way.

The truth was, he was starting to lose hope that anyone had even seen their emergency flare. With no idea how far out to sea they were, he had no way of knowing if they'd have any better luck in the morning with the orange flare.

He stared out at the ocean, noticing that it appeared a lot more normal than it had the last couple of nights. He was thankful for that, at least. He didn't know what exactly had happened, but he had a strong urge to sell the boat the second they docked at home. He could fish just as well in rivers and lakes.

He wished Sally was there, but at the same time, he was grateful she wasn't having to go through this with him. He could have even lost her during the storm, and he never could have lived with that.

He wondered how she was doing. She must be terribly worried by now, and he had no way to contact her and tell her he was all right.

Then again, he didn't even know *if* he was all right.

High above, a shooting star blazed through the sky. He stared at it and wished he could spend the night at home in bed with her. There was nowhere on earth he would rather be. If—*when*—he got home to her, he wouldn't take one moment with her for granted.

Dave muttered in his sleep. He tossed his head back and forth a couple of times, sweat beading on his forehead. Mark was worried about him. He was worried about his broken foot, too. He knew an injury like that was nothing to mess around with. He just hoped it wasn't getting infected. That was the last thing either of them needed to deal with.

At least the electrical systems seemed to be working fine now. All the lights were on. Unfortunately, the navigation system was apparently permanently burned out. At least they could move and they could broadcast their location. It was a definite improvement from the night before.

This night was quiet, but he could still hear the gentle lap of waves. Sound appeared to be carrying normally again. He couldn't yet wrap his brain around what exactly had been happening the last couple of days, but he was grateful things seemed to have returned to normal, relatively speaking, anyway. He thought about the brief conversation he'd had with Dave. The other had said that old sailors told weird stories about the area.

Devil's Triangle stories, he thought to himself.

He'd heard a few of them, but having practically grown up on the sea, he hadn't given them much thought. He knew just how treacherous the ocean could be and how fast storms could come up. There were a dozen reasons why a boat could vanish without having to make up crazy stories about it.

Like what happened to us.

He sat very still as that thought rattled around in his mind. Some people told weird stories about the area. Others just disappeared, so no one knew what their stories may have been.

What if they *were* missing? What if there were people out looking for them and they couldn't find *The Guardians*? What if they were lost forever and no one ever found them? His panic was returning a little bit and he took a deep breath to calm himself.

It was just silly superstition. His grandfather hadn't subscribed to it and neither did he.

But he couldn't explain what had happened to them. The darkness, the loss of lights, the complete, bizarre loss of navigation, the thick fog which came from nowhere and settled in so deeply he couldn't hear himself speak.

One by one, he came up with logical explanations for each of them. As they lost battery power, some of the lights failed before others, though he couldn't exactly explain the reason for that. The navigation had just been shot, possibly by a power surge. Terrible luck, but hey, it could happen. Fog occurred naturally all the time and had even been known to linger one place for hours if conditions were right. This particular fog was just worse than anything he'd ever encountered.

The only thing he couldn't explain was the darkness which had devoured all light and sound. Just remembering it spooked him again. He cleared his throat just to reassure himself that he could hear it.

He was being an idiot. Still, he had a strong urge to wake Dave, to ask him if he'd ever heard a story similar to theirs. Mostly, though, he just wanted to hear someone else's voice, to have reassurance that he wasn't alone.

Just as he was about to go shake Dave awake, he heard a creaking sound in the distance. He strained his ears, listening. It slowly grew louder. He stood up and thought he could see a light in the distance.

Excitement surged through him.

"Dave, wake up!" he called elatedly.

"What is it?" the other man asked groggily.

"I think it's another ship."

"Where?" Dave asked, instantly coming fully awake.

Mark pointed. There definitely was a light, and it was coming closer. He was certain he heard a shout.

Suddenly the quiet was ripped apart by a deafening roar. There was an explosion of fire and a hissing sound as something raced through the air toward them.

Dave threw himself forward off his chair, tackling Mark to the deck.

"Cannonball! They're shooting at us!"

11

"What the hell?" Mark gasped as pain exploded throughout his body.

There was an enormous splash a little distance past them as the cannonball hit the water.

"We have to get out of here!" Dave shouted, rolling off of him with a grunt. "Help me get up the ladder so I can get the engines started!"

Mark realized there wasn't time. Dave was the pilot, but in the time it would take them to get him up to the wheelhouse with his bad foot, another cannonball would strike them and they'd be sunk. Mark scrambled across the deck, grasped the ladder and barely made it up.

Another cannonball came whistling toward them just as he started the ship's engine. The grind of the engine shattered the night, but it wasn't loud enough to cover up the sound of the second cannonball splashing down much closer to them than the first.

"Hold on!" he shouted.

He gunned the engine and the boat thrust forward through the water, rapidly picking up speed.

Ahead and slightly to the left, he suddenly saw a flash of fire in the darkness. It wasn't that far off, and a second later a cannonball came from that direction and missed the boat by yards.

He shouted and jerked the wheel about.

"There's two ships!" Dave yelled up to him.

"I know!" he yelled back.

Both ships were running dark and silent and he had no real way of seeing them. All he could do was guesstimate as to where they were based on the direction the cannonballs appeared to be coming from.

"Cut our lights!" Dave shouted from the base of the ladder.

Mark scrambled to do that even as he tried to figure out just how far away from the second ship he'd turned the wheel.

The lights went out, plunging everything into utter darkness. Only the sound of their engine now gave away their location.

"Why are they shooting at us?" he called out. "And with cannonballs?"

He heard Dave grunting and cursing in Latin and in English. Moments later, his friend dragged himself up over the edge of the wheelhouse and collapsed on the ground by Mark's feet.

"Maybe they're shooting at each other and we just got in the way," he suggested with a gasp. "Old ships...cannonballs. I think we accidentally sailed into the middle of a reenactment. In any case, we need to get the hell out of here."

"I couldn't agree more," Mark said through gritted teeth.

There was a flash of light off to his right and another cannonball came their way. He yanked the steering wheel again as this one came even closer.

"I don't know where both ships are."

"Right now, they're at your nine and two o'clock, if that helps you any."

"Yes, thank you," Mark growled. "If they want us, they're going to have to catch us."

He opened the throttle all the way up and the boat accelerated, cutting through the water as it rushed forward. He flinched as cannons were simultaneously fired from both sides.

"Steady," Dave said.

"Who fires cannons at people?" Mark asked.

"Pirates."

"Pirates? That's crazy!"

"It's either that or overzealous reenactors. Personally, I don't want to stick around and find out."

Mark heard the sound of another incoming cannonball. He gritted his teeth and stayed the course. Seconds later, it splashed

78

down five yards to the front and right of his boat.

Were they still shooting at them?

He jerked the wheel involuntarily, sending the ship in a partial circle.

Great. Now I really do have no idea where I am, he realized.

He had never been so lost in his entire life, and with two enemies in the darkness trying to kill him, it was enough to make him want to start screaming and call for help.

There was no help coming, though. They were on their own. He wasn't sure what was happening or where the other ships were. What if he had just put them on a collision course with the second ship?

As if sensing his fear, Dave hissed at him suddenly.

"What?"

"Cut the engine!"

Mark immediately did as his friend asked, heart pounding. The ship fell silent but was still drifting forward. He could hear the water lapping at the hull. He strained eyes and ears, trying to locate their attackers. He could see Dave watching the ocean, obviously doing the same thing.

After a minute, Mark was about to say something when Dave held up his hand for silence. He must have heard something, given the way he cocked his head.

It was agony for Mark to remain so still. He couldn't help but wonder how their attackers managed to keep so silent. It felt as if they were completely alone, adrift on an empty sea. Yet he knew that couldn't be the case, so he continued to hold his tongue.

All of a sudden, Dave sucked in a hard breath. He grabbed hold of the back of Mark's seat, hauled himself up, turned on the engine, and threw the ship into reverse.

A shout from above caused Mark to look up. There above them towered a ship with tall sails. They had been within seconds of striking her broadside. More figures appeared on the deck high above them, silhouetted against flickering firelight.

Dave managed to turn the bow of *The Guardians* before

shifting out of reverse. The boat plowed forward, waves buffeting her bow. Dave fell back onto the ground and Mark grabbed wildly at the wheel.

Fire suddenly lit up the night sky and for that one moment, he caught a glance of both ships. He opened up the throttle and sped away as fast as he could. Cannons whistled through the air overhead.

There was a sickening crash as one tore through wood. For a terrible moment, he thought they'd been hit, but then he realized the ship they'd nearly rammed was the one in trouble.

Sweat poured down his forehead, burning his eyes and half blinding him, but he couldn't risk taking a hand off the wheel to wipe it away. Behind him, the two titans raged, and he could only hope that they became so obsessed with each other that he and Dave could escape.

He had the boat completely cranked up and going as fast as it could. He tried to focus on remaining on a straight heading. In the confusion and dark, with his heart racing and no navigational instruments working, it was harder than he'd ever imagined it could be. Still, he tried to keep his hands locked in the same positions relative to each other and prayed for the best.

Given the way the storm had tossed them around, not to mention the bizarre threat of cannonballs, he knew he should be grateful *The Guardians* was still even afloat, let alone capable of moving.

"Please hold together, girl," he whispered under his breath, trying to offer the ship whatever encouragement he could.

For a moment it seemed as though she responded with an extra burst of speed, lurching forward. He bit back a shout of triumph.

Suddenly, the ship slowed and he heard a terrible, grinding sound. He had no idea what it was, but it didn't sound good. Could it be the engine was giving up? Was it going to die on them? Before he could even think of the possible options available to him to keep that from happening, the ship slammed hard into something.

80

He and Dave were thrown forward as the ship's momentum abruptly ceased. They both smashed hard into the control console. Mark fell down beside Dave.

As he did so, he twisted, looking up. He somehow expected to see faces looking down on them, since he was certain they had just rammed into the other ship.

Thankfully, there was nothing staring down at them but the moon. He gazed at it for a moment, trying to comprehend what it meant. His vision went blurry for a moment before fading to black.

~

Sally woke, her heart pounding, shadows of another nightmare fading fast from her mind. She sat bolt upright, unsure for a moment where she was. Then she remembered she was in a hotel room waiting to hear that the coast guard had found and rescued Mark and Dave.

She checked her phone. It was still nighttime. There had been no calls or texts. She thought about getting up, but sleep still tugged at the corners of her mind, trying to pull her back down into darkness.

She couldn't remember much about her dream except that Mark was in terrible danger and someone was trying to kill him.

Her head was aching and throbbing so mercilessly that she finally got up to get a glass of water so she could take some aspirin.

Once she had done that, she sat back down on the bed and took several deep breaths. She closed her eyes and thought of Mark. She tried to picture him on the boat, tried to reach out to him with her mind and heart. She wanted him to know how much she loved him, how much she wanted him to come home.

It was crazy, but for a moment she thought she smelled his aftershave. She tried to breathe it in, wishing him there with her.

"I love you, Mark. Come back to me," she whispered into

the night.

She listened, as though she might actually hear him calling back to her. There was nothing, though.

She slipped back under the covers, laid down and prayed for sleep.

~

Mark felt as if he was falling, and it hurt more than he ever would have thought it could. Pain knifed through his temple. He blinked rapidly until he finally started getting his sight back. Slowly, the rest of his senses kicked in. He heard a horrible, wailing, grinding noise and the scent of smoke filled his nostrils.

"Turn off the engine," Dave gasped from somewhere next to him.

Mark somehow managed to drag himself up to his feet and reach for the engine. The moment he turned it off, the noise ceased. He just hoped they hadn't burned out the motor.

"What did we hit?" Mark asked, feeling as if he was not only moving and talking slowly, but also thinking slowly. "I don't see another ship."

"I don't know. It wasn't another ship," Dave said.

"Maybe we hit land or a reef or something," Mark said, his head pounding in agony as he tried to work it all out.

Land would be good, at least. They'd be able to find out where they were and get back home. He looked around, squinting, but only inky darkness greeted him.

"I don't know where we are," he admitted, his voice slurring as if he'd had one too many drinks.

Maybe I have a concussion, he thought.

"Are you bleeding, or am I?" Dave asked, his voice weak.

"What do you mean?"

"Can't you smell the blood?"

Blood?

He couldn't smell anything other than the spent engine, but

Mark touched his pounding temple and his fingers encountered something warm and sticky. It stung where he touched it and he grunted in pain.

"Apparently, I am," he said. "I must have hit my head. Are you okay?"

Dave didn't answer.

"Dave? You okay?" Mark called anxiously. His voice was loud enough to make his head ring.

The silence continued.

Panic filled his heart as he narrowed his gaze and stared down, trying desperately to locate his friend. "Dave?"

There was still no answer.

Mark dropped to his knees. That was when the scent of blood filled his nostrils.

12

Dave was bleeding badly from a shoulder wound. A piece of metal appeared to be lodged in it. His scalp was also bleeding, just as Mark's was. Since the head wound appeared superficial, Mark focused his attention on staunching the flow of blood from his friend's shoulder.

He ripped off the tattered remains of Dave's shirt and stuffed it against the wound. He couldn't see the metal well enough in the moonlight to risk trying to take it out. He didn't know how deep it was and he was afraid of making things worse.

"Come on, Dave. You're better at this stuff than I am," he muttered, wishing the priest would wake up.

Then again, it was probably better for Dave if he didn't, because Mark wasn't sure how he'd be able to handle the pain.

~

It was midmorning when Sally finally woke up. She rolled over and snatched up her phone. The only thing she'd missed was a text from her mother asking if she'd heard anything. She sent a brief text back letting her know the coast guard was still searching.

She called John, who had given her his direct number the day before. He answered on the second ring.

"Good morning," he said, sounding beyond tired.

"Anything?" she asked, though she could already tell by the weariness in his voice there was nothing new to report.

"No, nothing yet. We have every available man out looking."

She bit her tongue before she could demand to know why he wasn't out looking, too. Someone had to stay at the station and coordinate and handle other issues that came up. Logically she knew that even if in her heart, she wanted the whole U.S. Navy to converge on the area in the search.

"Mark has a few friends who have boats," she offered, belatedly realizing she should have immediately called and ask for their help in the search.

"While I appreciate the offer, I don't want anyone else out there we'd have to worry about," John said. "Let the experts do their jobs."

"Why? Is there something going on? Something you're not telling me? Some reason to worry more about ships getting lost today than at other times?"

"No, I'm just saying that we already have a lot of trained men out on the water and we don't need civilians getting in the way," he said, his voice hardening. "Especially emotional ones."

"Like me?"

She heard him sigh. "I wasn't purposefully making a comment about you. Obviously, you have every reason to be emotional. However, I would object strongly if you tried to take a boat out yourself in that mental state. The ocean can be treacherous enough for those who are calm and thinking clearly."

Mentally she told herself not to antagonize the man who was her best ally in this whole mess. If she did, she'd likely find herself banned from the station. That would be worse.

"I'll be there in a few minutes," she said.

"There's really no need. You know from your experience yesterday that there's absolutely nothing you can do here. It'd be best if you just went home to your family. I'll call the second I have anything to report."

"I can't go home to my family. Not without answers."

"Okay." He sighed. "I suppose I'll see you in a while."

She was grateful he didn't point out that she might never

have answers. She didn't need that kind of thinking right now. She had to think positively. She couldn't go her whole life not knowing what had happened to her husband, and she refused to have her daughters live with that uncertainty, either.

~

The dawn finally came. Mark greeted it with a wave of relief which swiftly gave way to consternation. The boat had indeed run aground on an island and not a reef.

The problem was, they had managed to run all the way up onto the dry ground. He climbed down and landed on the sand, which shifted slightly beneath his feet. The ship looked worn and battered. It was clear to see she'd been through a heck of a storm.

He began to walk around the hull, surveying the damage as he went. Finally, he came to the bow. There he discovered a jagged, gaping hole which was far too large to be repaired. He rubbed his temples with his fingers. After all they'd been through, they were now literally grounded. They weren't going anywhere.

Not in the boat, anyway.

He finished his visual inspection. He couldn't see what the entire hull looked like, but the gaping hole in the bow was enough of a problem all by itself.

He took a few minutes and looked for any other signs of life on the island. It wasn't large, so it didn't take long. The island was also flat and the vegetation that was present consisted of a lot of new growth and some older felled trees that had probably been felled by a storm at some point. There were hundreds of small, uninhabited islands and they'd managed to crash on one.

He climbed back onboard the boat. They had two flairs left and they were going to have to use them to summon help, since they weren't going to be able to go any farther. Hopefully a ship would pass their way soon and they'd be rescued.

Dave was awake and sitting up when he returned to the boat.

Mark forced a smile even though it was the last thing he felt like doing.

"How bad is it?" Dave asked.

"It's fine, great even, if we have plans to turn the ship into a waterfront tiki bar. The beach is nice."

Dave winced. "Grounded?"

"Permanently, I'd think it's safe to say."

"That's not what I wanted to hear."

"That's not what I wanted to say," Mark told him with a shrug. "Nevertheless, it is the truth. We've run aground on a small island."

"Any signs of life?"

"No."

"Any idea where we are?"

"An island."

"Brilliant. Thank you for your astute observation. Except there are only around 1700 of those in the Florida Keys," Dave said sarcastically.

"Aha! Right. But you're assuming we're still in the Keys," Mark countered. "After what we've been through, we could be anywhere."

"Remind me again why we're friends?"

"Because everyone needs one friend who will do idiotic things with you."

"Why do I have the feeling we're about to do an idiotic thing?" Dave asked.

"Experience," Mark said with a smirk.

He was trying to keep things as light as he could. Their circumstances were pretty grim, but it did neither of them any good to dwell on that. Sometimes the only difference between survival and death was a person's attitude.

"At least I think we escaped those ships," Dave said.

"Yeah, although I'd like to know who the heck they were and why they were shooting at us."

"Pirates, smugglers, something like that, I guess."

"With cannonballs. That's insane," Mark muttered.

"When that one guy shouted at us from the boat, did you hear what he was saying? It sounded like he was speaking in Spanish."

"No, I'm sorry. I was a little too busy panicking to notice."

"Pretty sure he was."

"You don't think we've drifted too far south and are close to Cuba, do you?"

"I hope not," Dave said fervently. "The Cuban military aren't exactly known for their hospitality."

"Well, sooner or later someone is going to come along and we need to be ready to signal to them when they do."

"I guess so."

"You *guess* so? What other options do we really have?"

Dave shook his head. "None, but I'm trying to figure out one."

"Well, while you're busy doing that, I'm going to get us something to eat," Mark said.

He went downstairs to raid the food stores. Instead, he found himself in his bedroom, sitting on the edge of the bed taking deep breaths in and out. He felt as if he was going to be sick. He suddenly realized his own head injury was making him a little dizzy and off-balance. It was more than that, though, and he struggled to put into words how he was feeling.

He finally realized that the best way to describe it was *shock*. So many bizarre things had come at them in the last two days and it was starting to take a toll. The realization that they were stuck on this island until someone found them wasn't helping. He couldn't keep from thinking about the movie *Castaway* and wonder if, like Tom Hank's character, he'd start treating inanimate objects like friends.

Not if I can keep Dave alive, he thought doggedly.

He shuddered. He hadn't let himself think about it before, but now reality was confronting him head on. Dave now desperately needed medical attention for a variety of things— and he needed it fast. It was only a matter of time, hours maybe, before infection started to set in. Mark still needed to figure out how best to remove the metal from Dave's shoulder.

He retrieved his phone from the nightstand and checked it. There was still no service. He turned it off to save battery before putting it back.

~

The day dragged by with mind-numbing slowness. Sally sat in John's office, leaving her chair only to use the restroom or get herself more coffee. At lunch, he brought her a sandwich, and once again at dinner. They ate in silence. She wasn't sure which of them was more tense and worried.

With every report that came in, she started to her feet, only to sink back down in despair when there was no news. Finally, John sent her back to the hotel for the night, promising to call her the second he heard anything at all.

~

As darkness fell, Mark became more worried. He hadn't been able to spot any passing ships all day. They had agreed not to waste their one daytime flair. They would only fire it if and when they saw a ship out on the water. He was thinking they should save the nighttime one, as well, until they heard something or saw lights.

Earlier, he'd explored part of the island. As he'd thought, it appeared to be deserted. There was some vegetation, but most of it didn't look like old growth. As Dave had said, there were nearly a couple of thousand islands in the Keys, and most of them were uninhabited. He just wished he knew how close this one was either to a populated island or the mainland itself.

"So, the bar we're planning on setting up here, are we going to serve food?" Dave asked.

"Pub grub, of course."

"Great. In that case, I'll take a hamburger."

"I think I can wrangle you up a peanut butter and jelly

sandwich."

"Sold."

"You're a cheap date."

"Just because I'm cheap doesn't mean I'm easy," Dave retorted.

Mark couldn't help but chuckle as he went downstairs to get them both sandwiches. At least Dave hadn't lost his sense of humor.

~

Sally spent the night tossing and turning before finally returning to the Coast Guard Station in the morning. The day slowly crept by, just as bad as the past two had been. She could tell John was losing hope, but at least he tried to stay upbeat in front of her. She wanted to hear something that gave her hope, anything.

She spent yet another sleepless night at the hotel and was once again getting ready to head to the station. She sat down on the edge of the bed and relistened to the last message Mark had left her. She closed her eyes and listened to his voice, trying to imagine he was there with her. When it was done, she pulled up the last picture she'd taken of him, one of him playing with the girls.

Her phone rang, startling her out of her reverie.

"Hello, Sally? This is John. How are you this morning?"

"Aside from some new gray hairs, about as well as I can be expected to be, I guess. Do you have an update?" she asked.

There was a long pause and for a moment she thought the call had dropped. "Hello?"

"Sorry. I hate to be the one to have to tell you this, but we still haven't found anything and they're officially calling off the search."

"What? No!" she screamed.

"At this point, without new data to go on, there's really nothing else we can do. I'm very sorry. If you need any--"

The phone slipped from her nerveless fingers and crashed onto the floor. A moment later, she was on her knees beside it, her body wracked by great, heaving sobs.

13

Going home was one of the hardest things that Sally had ever had to do in her life. It felt like a defeat, like she was somehow admitting that her husband was gone.

He wasn't gone. She knew he wasn't. She could feel that in her heart. She just had to keep the faith no matter who else had lost theirs.

Somehow, he'd come back to her.

As she back drove to the house, she spent some time on the phone with her mom, Eva. The older woman was deeply sympathetic, but Sally could tell she'd given up hope. She didn't say so, but it was there in her voice.

"We'll drop the girls back at your house in the morning," Eva said. "To give you a little time."

To grieve.

Her mother didn't have to say the words aloud.

"Thank you," Sally said. "I need to get some sleep tonight and I'll be able to be there for them in the morning."

"When do you plan to tell them about Mark?"

"I'm going to tell them he got called away on business for a few days and he'll be back as soon as he can."

There was a lengthy pause. Finally, her mom asked, "Do you really think that's wise?"

Sally didn't hesitate. "Yes, I do. There's no use worrying them needlessly at this point."

Her mom fell silent again. She didn't have to speak, Sally could feel her objection in the silence.

"He's not gone, and I won't tear the girls up with fear and grief when there's no reason to do so. I just need to give him a little longer to find his way home to us."

92

"How much longer?" Eva asked.

"As long as it takes." Her words came out firm, but her stomach fluttered.

"Okay. In the meantime, it would probably be a good idea if you went and had a talk with Aunt Pamela."

"I'm not crazy, Mom!" Sally snapped.

"Of course you're not crazy, Dear, but you are going through a trauma. She's very good with helping people through rough patches."

Aunt Pamela, her mom's younger sister, was a therapist. She was very good at her job—seeing people through their *rough patches*. She was so good that she could even take on family members as patients without losing her aloof attachment.

Which was exactly why Aunt Pamela was not a person she'd ever want to talk to about any of this. The last thing she needed was for Aunt Pamela to stare at her with those cold, dead eyes of hers and tell her how to run her life.

"I'm fine, Mom. I've got you and Dad to help me, and that's all I need."

"If you say so, dear. Just remember, you can get professional help if you need it. It's right at your fingertips."

"Thanks."

Her mom meant well, and she supposed she should be grateful for that.

"Is there anything else we can do?"

"No, Mom. Thanks. I'm just about home now and I need to get settled in. I'll call you when I wake up in the morning."

"Okay, love you, sweetheart."

"Love you, too."

Sally ended the call with a heavy sigh. She was still about fifteen minutes from home, but she couldn't handle speaking any more about Aunt Pamela or whether she was doing the right thing with the kids. Sometimes in a crisis, the most important thing to do was make up your mind and not let others try to change it for you.

Mark had taught her that and so many other things as well.

93

She could really use his strength at the moment. Wherever he was, though, he needed hers even more. She would be strong for both of them until he was back in her arms.

Tears stung her eyes, but she refused to let them fall. This was not a surrender, or even a retreat. This was her holding down the fort for him.

For all of them.

~

When she finally made it home and into the house, she was completely ready to collapse. She was certain if she didn't set an alarm, that she would sleep for a week. As appealing as that sounded, she had too much to do.

For one thing, she had to make several phone calls in the morning, starting with Mark's assistant at work. They were probably wondering why he hadn't checked in and would be starting to get really worried. By that same token, she realized she should call Dave's church and let them know why he wasn't back yet.

There were probably other calls she should make, but her head began throbbing just trying to think about it. She made it to the bedroom and started to undress. She was halfway through when she felt all her strength leave her at once and she sat down heavily on the bed.

The days of uncertainty were taking their toll. This was exactly what she didn't want to put the girls through if she could avoid it. Her stomach clenched and she couldn't decide if she was hungry or just stressed out. She'd only nibbled erratically at food the last three days. She was probably hungry.

She managed to get into her pajamas and then stumbled to the kitchen. She yanked open the refrigerator, looking for something even remotely healthy. The siren song of cookie dough ice cream in the freezer was nearly overwhelming, but she knew that wouldn't help her keep her strength up.

Nothing else looked even remotely appealing. Still, she

forced herself to take some cheese and deli meat out of the refrigerator drawer. She didn't even bother with bread. Instead she just took off the plastic and stacked slices of meat between cracker-sliced bits of cheese.

She got several bites in before her stomach rumbled angrily. She wrapped up the food and put it back in the refrigerator and then headed back to the bedroom.

For just a moment, the sight of her bedroom made everything feel normal. It was as though if she listened hard enough, she could hear the shower running and Mark singing from within.

"He's not dead," she whispered as she sat down on the edge of the bed.

~

The next morning, she was up and dressed with her makeup done and a fake smile plastered on her face. Her parents arrived with her daughters Emma and Jayne. The girls ran into the kitchen and threw their arms around her shouting, "Mama!"

She hugged them tightly and kissed the tops of both their heads. "Did you have fun at Grandma and Grandpa's?" she asked.

"Yes, we had ice cream every day!" Jayne squealed.

"Every day?" Sally asked, sounding impressed. "That's a lot of ice cream!"

"Where's Daddy?" Emma asked suddenly.

It was the moment of truth.

She squatted down so she could look them both in the eyes. "Daddy unexpectantly had to go on a business trip. He'll be gone for a little while, but hopefully not too long. He said to tell you both he loved you and to give you big hugs and kisses."

"When will he get back?" Jayne asked.

"We don't know just yet. Soon," Sally said.

She glanced up at her parents, who were frowning and shaking their heads slightly. It was clear they didn't approve.

They might have given up hope, but she hadn't yet. And she wasn't going to. She needed to keep the pain and uncertainty away from Emma and Jayne as long as she could.

Hopefully, it would be long enough.

~

Mark ripped off the last cabinet door inside the boat. One by one, they had all been sacrificed to make fires. He had managed to catch some more fish earlier and he was going to cook them. His mouth was watering just thinking about it.

They had been stranded on the island for a week now and he'd had time to explore the whole thing. There was nothing in the way of wildlife or fruit, which left him having to fish for their lives.

All his life, he had only fished for sport and pleasure. The activity took on a whole new meaning and an entirely different feel when it was the only way they could keep from starving to death. Every fish that got away felt like one more nail in his coffin.

Survival had become a real, tangible thing, and he vowed if he made it through this, he would never again take anything in his life for granted. He threw the wooden door off the boat and then jumped down beside it. Then he picked it up and walked the short distance down the beach to where Dave was set up with the best view of the horizon.

The other man wasn't looking well. His foot was healing, albeit slowly, but the wound in his shoulder was festering. Together, they'd removed the metal shard which had impaled him days earlier. Mark had tried to clean it as best he could and was faithfully applying antibiotic cream. It wasn't enough, and they both knew it.

Mark tossed the door onto the fire, which began to hungrily lick at the edges of the wood. He pulled a small, folding Swiss Army knife from his pocket and a tiny, airplane-sized bottle of whiskey from his other pocket.

"How are you doing?" Mark asked, carefully eyeing his friend.

"Worse than I look," Dave said, his voice shaking slightly.

"We can't have that," Mark said, trying to keep his tone light. The specter of losing Dave was hanging over his head. He knew that if they didn't do something drastic soon, in another day or two, the priest would be dead.

He crouched down and carefully removed the bandages from Dave's shoulder, scowling as he surveyed the white puss oozing from the wound.

He shook his head.

"You never can do anything the easy way, can you?" he asked. "Always got to make it difficult."

Dave snorted. "Why would I want to make things easy on you?"

"I'm not going to lie to you. This is going to hurt. A lot."

"I'm not going to lie to you. I'm going to be cursing at you. A lot."

"As long as you bless me later, Father," Mark said.

"Let's get the cursing over so we can get to the blessing part, then, why don't we?"

Mark poured a little of the whiskey into Dave's wound. The priest screamed and Mark did his best to ignore the stream of words pouring out of him as he took the knife and thrust the tip into the fire, heating it up. Not only would the blaze sterilize the instrument, but it would also make it so it would slice through flesh like butter.

"Okay, here we go," he warned as he took the blade from the fire.

Mark took a deep breath and then shoved the knife into the wound in Dave's shoulder. His friend screamed and immediately passed out, which was a mercy for both of them. Mark set about cutting out black, rotted chunks of flesh. The heat from the metal cauterized the wound as he worked so he didn't have to deal with blood. The stench of the burning flesh turned his stomach and nearly made him pass out, but he did

97

what he could to breathe through his mouth.

When he was finished, he poured more of the alcohol into the wound to flush it out. Finished with that, he liberally applied antibiotics before bandaging it back up.

As soon as he was done, he got up and walked a short distance away. His knees were shaking and eventually buckled. As he crashed onto the sand he began to vomit. That was the most horrible thing he'd ever had to do and he knew it would stay with him for the rest of his life. However long that was.

~

It was three hours before Dave woke up. In that time, Mark had cleaned up and cooked the rest of the fish he'd caught.

When Dave finally opened his eyes he groaned and wrinkled his nose.

"When we get back home, I don't ever want to see another fish again, much less eat one."

"You're preaching to the choir. How are you feeling?"

"Better, thank you. I think you burned all the toxins out of me."

"That was the idea."

"You know, I think that--"

Dave abruptly stopped talking. He tilted his head slightly, staring fixedly at something beyond Mark's left shoulder.

"What is it?" Mark asked.

"It's a boat!"

14

Mark squinted, looking in the direction Dave was pointing. There, bobbing up and down on the water, was indeed a boat.

"Shoot the flare!" Dave said.

Mark scrambled for their pile of supplies, retrieved the daytime flare gun and fired it, sending the plume of smoke high into the sky. He held his breath for a moment, his eyes fixed on the ship. Slowly, she turned, coming to bear on them.

"She saw our flare!" he shouted, tears streaming down his cheeks. "She's coming!"

Dave began praying fervently in Latin.

Together, they watched with growing excitement as the ship drew closer. It was a small ship, and eventually they could make out what appeared to be its sole occupant.

"It must be a fishing boat," Mark mused.

"Don't you dare say *fish.*"

"I don't know, Dave. It looks pretty old."

"It could be the boat Saint James and Saint John were in when the Lord called them to be apostles and I wouldn't care. We're saved! That's all that matters to me right now."

As the boat came closer, Mark realized it wasn't even anything as grand as a fishing boat.

It was a rowboat.

His consternation quickly gave way to excitement. If the man was on a rowboat, that meant either the man's ship was nearby or else civilization was.

Either way it was the best news ever.

~

Sally was having lunch out with her friend Meredith. She hadn't wanted to go, but everyone—including her parents--had been bothering her about getting back into her life. People appeared to be worried that she was going to become some sort of recluse.

The truth was, she wasn't yet ready to talk about Mark with anyone.

Still, she understood everyone's concern, which was why, against her better judgment, she'd finally agreed to have lunch with Meredith. It was turning out to be an even bigger mistake than she'd thought it would be.

"You need to have a funeral for Mark," Meredith stressed, reaching out to grasp Sally's hand. "I know how difficult this has been for you, but you've got to let him go. Everyone needs closure."

Sally blinked at her, wondering if she could possibly be hearing the other woman correctly.

"Excuse me?"

"A funeral. A celebration of Mark's life. It's time to lay him to rest figuratively, even if you can't literally. You'll never be able to get on with your life if you don't."

Sally spoke through a clenched jaw. "That's not happening. They've never found the ship *or* the bodies, or even any wreckage. Besides, I feel in my heart that he's alive. You know that feeling you get, where it's almost as if you can sense the other person? When you know they're in trouble? Mark and I have always had that. He's not dead. I'd know it in my heart if he was."

Meredith gazed at her sympathetically. "Honey, you're deluding yourself," she said, squeezing Sally's hand. "Which is understandable, especially given the circumstances. Heaven knows I've been there. Not with the dead husband part, but with the deluding myself about my husband part."

Sally couldn't believe her ears. Meredith's husband was a womanizer who cheated on her frequently. And yet every time he came back begging at her door, Meredith forgave him and took him back, saying this time when he promised not to do it again, he was being serious and he would keep his word. The fact that she was comparing their messed up existence to what was happening to Sally now with Mark missing was insane.

"I'm not holding a funeral until I have a reason to do so, and that won't happen until I have a body," Sally said. "That's the end of it. Can we talk about something else, please?"

"Look, this isn't just about you. A lot of people loved him and need the opportunity to grieve and say goodbye. The fact that you would deny all of us that, well, it's not fair," Meredith said. "You need--"

"Not *fair*? You want to know what's not fair? It's not *fair* that you're lying, cheating husband is alive and with you while my Mark, the kindest, noblest husband in the world is…missing. Where is the justice there?"

"How dare you say that to me?"

Sally burst into irrational laughter, unable to contain herself. It was the only response she had for such an insane question.

"Stanley is--"

"Stanley is a pig," Sally spat. "You've said so yourself on many, many occasions. What did he buy you this time to make you look the other way and tell yourself he's not so bad? And who's been there every time he's made a fool of you? Who held you when you cried, and helped you dig your self-esteem out of the garbage? Huh?"

She paused for a moment, frowning at her friend. "Oh, that's right. *Me*. Now when I need your support, you're so quick to tell me *I* am the delusional one. Mark is *not dead*, and unless I see his body, there will be no funeral."

Sally stood abruptly and stormed out of the restaurant. She could hear Meredith blustering behind her, spouting something unintelligible.

It didn't matter. They were through. Meredith was a taker and always had been. Sally's only mistake had been in thinking if she someday needed Meredith's support, she would get it.

That had *so* not happened.

She managed to make it to her car and sat for a moment, clenching the steering wheel with one hand and wiping angry tears from her eyes.

Her phone rang and Sally scowled. If Meredith was calling her to try to have the final word, then she had another thing coming.

She glanced at the screen, but it wasn't Meredith.

It was John calling.

She eagerly snatched it up and punched the button to connect the call.

"Did you find him?" she asked breathlessly.

"No, but we found…something. Can you come down to the office?"

"Yes. I'm ten minutes away. I'll be there as fast as I can."

She sped out of the parking lot, skidding slightly as she turned onto the street.

What could they have found? Why hadn't he just told her over the phone? Hope and fear vied for dominance in her heart as she raced toward the Coast Guard station. She came to a red light and nearly ran it before slamming on her brakes at the last second.

Breathe. Breathe. You won't do Mark or the girls any good if you get yourself killed driving like a maniac, she told herself.

It seemed like the longest drive of her life, with her mind and heart racing faster than the car's engine. She finally reached her destination and a young man in uniform escorted her into John's office.

John was sitting behind his desk but immediately stood when she entered.

"What is it? What have you found?" Sally eagerly burst out, unable to contain the words for even a second more.

John looked perplexed, as if he was trying to find the words he needed.

She didn't understand what could be so difficult that he couldn't just spit it out. Suddenly, a gleam on the wall caught her eye. There was a picture of *The Guardians*, her husband's boat, hanging alongside all the other pictures of boats lost at sea.

Her mouth gaped open and her stomach lurched.

John turned his head, saw what she was looking at and quickly strode over to the wall. He tore the picture off the wall, crumpled it into a ball and dropped it in a trashcan.

Then he heaved a sigh and met her gaze. "It appears we found the boat."

There was something peculiar about the way he said it, as if it was a question and not a statement.

"What do you mean *appears*? Did you find it or not?"

"It seems to be the boat."

"I don't understand. How hard can it be? It's either Mark's boat or it's not," she said, getting frustrated.

And if it was Mark's boat, where was Mark?

"We…I…it would be helpful if you could positively identify it."

She had the oddest reaction to his words, an icy finger flickering up her spine.

Identifying the boat is a lot different than identifying a body, she reminded herself.

"Where is it?"

"It's on an island about 45 minutes from here. If you wouldn't mind taking a short journey, I'd like you to accompany me there."

"That's fine. Whatever I have to do," she hastened to say.

"Great. We'll go by helicopter. We can leave whenever you're ready."

"I'm ready now."

He nodded and escorted her out of his office and down the hall. Five minutes later, they were in a helicopter, heading out to sea.

Mark felt uneasy as he watched the shore retreat from view. The tiny rowboat they were in was not something he'd ever cheerfully venture onto the ocean in. Hopefully, the man's fishing boat was nearby. He'd only spoken Spanish, but they had managed to communicate that they needed help. That was about all, which was frustrating. Hopefully it was enough.

Fortunately, the man had agreed to take them off the island. Still, something wasn't sitting entirely right with Mark about the situation. He just couldn't put his finger on it.

Mark also didn't like leaving their boat behind, even if it was beached. He should have been rejoicing that someone had found them and was rescuing them, but something niggling deep inside him was extremely uneasy about the whole situation. Maybe it was the fact that the small vessel they were in felt as if it could capsize at any moment. Maybe it was the fact that their rescuer kept staring at them in a strange way. Then again, maybe it was just that he was terrified of what they were going to find out about Dave's physical wounds when they got back to civilization and checked him into the hospital.

Mark had done everything he could for him, but he needed professional care. What if what he'd done wasn't enough?

Every time he thought about it, he got queasy and felt a horrible sense of guilt. After all, it was his boat that had malfunctioned in the first place.

He took a deep breath. They would get through this somehow. And being rescued by this man was a good first step.

"Don't worry about it," Dave muttered.

"Worry about what?" he asked.

"None of this is your fault. You did everything right. We're going to get back in time to save my life, given how this infection is spreading. Timing is everything, you know."

"Are you reading my mind again?"

"No, just quieting my own. I've been telling myself this was an accident and I shouldn't blame myself."

Mark shook his head. "You're unbelievable. The last person you should be blaming for anything is yourself."

"Same goes for you," Dave said doggedly.

"I'll stop if you do."

104

"Deal."

"Do you think we can trust this guy? He seems pretty squirrely," Mark whispered, changing the subject. The man didn't act as if he understood any English, but Mark didn't want to take any chances on it.

"I hope so, but it's not like we really have much of a choice in the matter."

"I know we don't. It's just that I'm feeling really uneasy for some reason."

"I hear you. If it helps, I've got the flare gun with the last flare loaded into it in my bag."

"Great," Mark said, rolling his eyes. "If it comes to that, just make sure you hit the guy and not the boat. We don't need another boat going down with us in it."

"Technically, the first one didn't sink," Dave pointed out.

"Thanks. That makes me feel loads better."

Dave shrugged. "At least it's accurate."

"You know, for a guy whose job is all about faith, you sure are monotonously logical and precise."

"It's a gift."

Suddenly, the man hissed something in Spanish and hunched his shoulders. He lifted his oars out of the water and cocked his head to the side as though he were listening to something.

Mark's heart began to pound. He wanted to ask Dave what the man had said, but he figured he had gotten the gist of it. The man wanted them to be silent because he had heard something.

Whatever that something was, it was clearly making the man nervous and fearful. After everything they'd recently been through, Mark figured the odds were decent it should make them nervous and fearful, too.

Unless he's not a fisherman, but some kind of drug runner afraid of the authorities. In which case, we shouldn't be quiet, but rather make as much noise as possible, he thought to himself.

Making his decision, he filled his lungs with air, preparing to shout as loud as he could. At the last moment, though, something stopped him. He thought about the pirates who had attacked Dave and him. They had easily been able to outrun the ancient ships in *The Guardians*, but they would be sitting ducks in this old dinghy.

He strained his eyes and ears, trying to discover what it was that had sent their rescuer into such a state of alert. After several seconds, he still hadn't heard or seen anything. Then, for just a moment, he thought he caught the sound of a motor. It was there one moment and then gone again. He glanced back at the tiny island they had left behind, wondering again if they had done the right thing.

The rays of the sun began to pierce through the clouds and mercilessly beat down on them.

"I forgot my hat," he said suddenly.

"What?" Dave asked, raising his eyebrows.

"My hat. We left in such a hurry, I forgot to grab it."

"You can get a new hat."

"Sally gave me that hat."

"Sally will be so happy to see you she'll buy you a hundred new hats."

Dave was right about that. He'd lost count of how long they'd been on the island, but there was no doubt Sally would be so happy to see him she'd cheerfully get him another hat.

And he would never again go fishing without her.

Scratch that. He would never go fishing again at *all*.

~

"Where are we going?" Sally asked as she stared at the ocean below.

"It's a small, privately-owned island in the Berry Island chain near the Bahamas," John said, his voice coming through on the headset she was wearing. "A philanthropist bought it a couple of years ago with the idea of turning it into an exotic animal hospital and sanctuary. There is a team on the island right now surveying it. They're the ones who brought it to our attention this morning."

"Brought what to your attention?" she asked.

He didn't answer but merely shook his head. She still couldn't figure out what it was that he didn't want to tell her, but she was certain there was something.

By the time they finally landed on the island, she was feeling completely sick to her stomach, both from the motion of the helicopter and the anxiety regarding what she might find.

She didn't have a single second to catch her breath. The moment she stepped foot on solid ground, she was hurried into a waiting Jeep, which took off bumping and jolting over the uneven ground. When it finally came to a stop, she half-fell out of it, immediately dropping to her hands and knees before she proceeded to throw up.

"You okay?" John asked her, sympathy in his voice.

"Not even a little bit," she said, clutching her stomach and worrying that another bout might come on any moment.

"I'm sorry. I've got something you can take for the motion sickness before we head back."

"That would be good. Thank you. So, what did you drag me all the way out here to show me?" she asked.

"It's just about thirty yards down from here. Are you okay to walk?"

She figured she could walk ninety feet, even if her legs were wobbly. Besides, at the moment, that sounded a whole lot more appealing than the thought of having to get right back onto a moving vehicle. At least out here she could breathe fresh air.

They moved a few feet through what looked like brush and trees which had been recently cleared away.

"The workmen who were clearing this area found something very unusual and called us," John said.

"You're being very vague. What exactly is it that they found?" she asked, growing even more frustrated with his evasiveness.

He stopped in front of a fat, squat palm and then turned and looked at her. "This," he said, pulling the fronds of the palm tree back so she could see past it.

There, in the middle of the bushes, was an old, weathered boat. She took a hesitant step forward, her heart quickening as she recognized it. Without a shadow of a doubt she knew it was her husband's boat, *The Guardians*--only there was an ancient tree growing right up through the middle of it.

15

"Mark!" Sally shouted and lunged forward, nearly tripping over some roots on the ground. She made it to the boat. The letters were faded, but she could still brush her fingers over the name *The Guardians* on the ship.

"Mark! Dave!" she screamed frantically, hoping beyond hope they would hear her.

There was no answer.

The boat was in terrible shape. She struggled to understand exactly what it was she was staring at. The whole thing was filthy. Half the windows were broken out. There were layers of dirt and sand and grime caked all over it. Trees were growing all around it, and besides the large tree in the middle, there were two others also growing *through* it. Cobwebs hung thick over the whole thing.

She didn't care if what she was seeing was impossible. She had to get on board and look around. She needed to find her husband and his best friend.

"Help me!" she shouted to John, who had hung back when she'd run toward the boat.

He came forward slowly, a look of awe on his face. "They told me," he said. "But seeing it this way is something else entirely."

"Help me up," she said, gripping the side of the boat.

He shook his head. "I don't think it's safe to go onboard, Sally. The boards are rotting through. You could hurt yourself."

"You can't stop me!" she snapped. "So either help me get up there or get out of the way."

He laced his fingers together and gave her a boost up. She managed to swing her body over the side of the boat and roll to a standing position. Cobwebs caught in her hair as she hurried toward the stairs leading below deck. She brushed them away but didn't slow her pace until she put her foot on the top step and it creaked.

"Careful!" John called, coming up behind her. "That wood looks like it's rotted out. One wrong step and your foot will go right through."

She clung tightly to the handrail as she descended, carefully testing each step before putting her weight on it. The last step cracked and shattered, but held long enough for her to get past it.

She had been in that hallway a hundred times in the past, yet it felt completely alien now. The stench of decay filled the air and there was a thick layer of dirt covering everything. None of this made sense.

Her heart pounded as she turned and headed for the master bedroom where Mark stayed when he was out on his fishing trips. She had no idea what had happened here or the how or why of it, but she was terrified of what she was going to find.

"Mark?" she called even though she knew in her heart he wasn't there.

The second she stepped foot in the room, she knew it was indeed her husband's boat, despite its ancient appearance. Everything was exactly as she remembered it except for the many years of decay which had set in. She could even make out a faint tropical floral pattern on the sheets, something Mark had objected to but she had insisted on.

She wanted to sit on the edge of the bed as she had so many times, to connect in some way to her husband, but the grime covering it repulsed her. She glanced at the chair in the room and stiffened. With a cry of agony, she rushed over and snatched up the hat that was sitting upon it. Just like everything else in the room, it was old and weathered, but she still would have known it anywhere.

Her pulse raced. Why was it here and Mark was not? He wore it constantly when on his fishing trips. His lucky hat, he'd called it.

She turned to show John the hat.

"This is Mark's favorite hat! I gave it to him as a gift for his birthday one year and he always wore it fishing. Where is my husband and what happened to this boat?" she demanded.

He shook his head and ran a hand across his jaw. "I wish I knew. I can't explain what happened to the boat. I just know scientifically it's been here at least one-hundred-and-fifty years. That's roughly how old the tree growing through the center of it looks. It had to have been beached here. There's a gash in the hull, so there was no way the boat would be seaworthy after that. Then the trees grew up around it. It defies reason, but this seems to be the same boat that went missing only a few weeks ago."

"It *is* the same boat," she said through clenched teeth.

"I agree with you. The surveying party was shocked to find the technology on board the ship was so modern. That's why they called us in."

"Where are Mark and Dave?"

He held out his hands in a helpless gesture. "They haven't found any signs of graves or skeletons here on the island. Assuming they were stranded here at the same time the boat was, it's possible they found a way off the island."

"A hundred and fifty years ago?" she asked, struggling to wrap her head around it.

"I know it sounds crazy, but, look around you. Crazy is pretty much all we've got at the moment."

All the weeks of uncertainty, of not knowing anything, and now they had found the ship. But instead of getting answers, all she had were more mysteries.

It was too much. Her legs suddenly gave out and she landed hard on the edge of the grimy, ancient bed. Tears of pain and frustration erupted. Since they had called off searching for the ship, she hadn't allowed herself to really and truly cry. Somehow, deep inside, she felt that if she cried, she'd be admitting he was gone and she'd never see him again.

111

She wasn't ready to do that.

That's why she wouldn't hold a funeral. A funeral implied finality, and there was nothing final about any of this.

Now, however, she didn't know what to think anymore. All of this was so far beyond her realm of imagination. None of it made any sense, and she could no longer hold back the waves of fear and doubt assuaging her. She was vaguely aware of John's presence hovering nearby. He stood silently with her for a few moments before heading down the corridor toward the second bedroom, the one Dave would have been using.

She didn't know how long it was before he came back.

He stood in the doorway for a moment before finally speaking. "I'm sorry, but we should go now."

She looked up at him, finding it hard to focus on his face through the tears. "Go where? What can we possibly do now?" she asked. "We can't just leave. We haven't found Mark and Dave."

"I wish I had the answers, but I promise, this is not over. I will help you figure out what happened here if it's within my power to do so."

Within my power to do so.

Slowly, she looked around at their surroundings. What had the power to do this? And how could they possibly hope to understand it?

"Where do you think they went?" she asked miserably. "And please don't say you wish you knew."

He scowled. "Okay. If they made it to this island with the boat, I think they left it shortly afterward. Maybe someone found them and took them to the mainland."

"What makes you think they weren't here for very long?"

"All the cabinet doors have been removed. That suggests to me they needed wood for a fire. If they were really here before the trees grew up, that was probably their best source of wood. But they didn't take out the drawers or start tearing apart the ship. They would have known there was no way they could patch the hull and make the ship seaworthy again. I think if they had been on the island for a longer period of time, they would have scavenged more of the boat for firewood or to build better lodgings or something."

"You mean like Robinson Crusoe?"

"Yes, something of that nature."

She glanced at the nightstand next to the bed. John was right. The drawer was still in it. The wood was warped, but she managed to open the drawer. Inside, she found some paper with writing on it. She carefully pulled it out and unfolded the pages. The writing was faint because of age and the paper was brittle. There wasn't enough light coming into the cabin for her to make out any of the words, but her heart skipped a beat as she recognized her husband's handwriting.

"Mark wrote this," she said, her voice trembling.

"He did? Maybe he explained what happened." John asked eagerly.

"I can't read it in here."

"It's past time for us to go, anyway."

She got up, clutching the papers, even as she worried about damaging them. Mark had written whatever was on them and she needed to read it, no matter what it was. Intuitively, she felt there was nothing left for her to find on the boat anyway, which made leaving it a little easier for her.

"What's going to happen to the ship?" she asked.

"We need to figure that out," John admitted. "We're going to have a team go over it in detail to try to find out everything they can about it and what happened to it. Then we can discuss what to do with it."

"You said it will never be seaworthy again."

"That's true," he confirmed.

"So, what are the options?" she asked.

"I don't know just yet. I'm just taking this one step at a time for now."

"Nobody is going to believe me," she murmured as they made their way to the stairs.

He glanced at her with a grimace. "About that. At least for

now, you might not want to share this finding with anyone."

"Why not?"

"As you pointed out, it's a pretty fantastic tale. Just give me a little time to try and understand what happened scientifically before you share this with anyone."

She shook her head. "The last thing I need is people thinking I've gone crazy, but you want me to keep all this a secret? I mean, if I can't talk about this to someone, I am actually going to go crazy. I can't just let this spin around and around in my head. I need someone I can talk it out with."

"I might know someone you can talk to. A friend."

"If you're about to say that they're a therapist or something like that, I'm going to shut you down right now."

"No, no. She's a writer. She specializes in these kinds of things."

"What *kinds of things?*" she asked as she carefully began to ascend the rotted stairway.

"Things which appear to have no natural explanation."

"Such as?"

She could hear him sigh as she made it up the last stair.

Suddenly, she heard a large cracking sound. She turned around just in time to see the stairs collapse underneath John and send him falling backward.

She shouted as he hit the deck beneath. "John, are you okay?"

He didn't answer.

Panic raced through her.

She turned and screamed at the top of her lungs. "Help! Please help! John's been hurt!"

A minute later, three men raced over, climbed up on top of the boat and she directed them to the collapsed stairs. Just as they got there, she heard John groan and she breathed in relief.

"You okay?" one of the guys yelled down to him.

"Nothing's broken, I don't think. If someone could throw me down a rope, that would be great," John said.

Sally stepped back out of the way, letting the others take

114

charge. She stood thinking as they worked out the best way to get John back up onto the deck. They managed the feat in short order. In just a couple of minutes, they were settled into the jeep, rattling and bouncing back to the helicopter.

~

She and John were silent for the entire return trip, each busy with their own thoughts. It wasn't until they'd made it back to the station and were in his office with the door closed that he finally turned to her.

"Promise me you won't tell other people about what we saw today, at least until we can figure out what's really going on."

It was a tall order. Then again, who could she really tell? It wasn't as if anyone would believe her. She thought about Meredith and some of her other friends. In general, they weren't the most open-minded people.

"Who would I tell? I don't want people to think I'm crazy," she admitted.

"I'd prefer not to be called that, either," John said.

"But people will believe you. The guys you work with have seen it, too."

"Yeah. Still, we don't like to advertise these kinds of things."

"Unnatural things."

"Things that *appear* unnatural," he corrected her.

"And this author friend of yours--"

"Janis. She's been doing research for years."

"On what, exactly?"

"The Devil's Triangle."

16

Sally stared open-mouthed at John for a long moment.

"You mean the Bermuda Triangle?" she finally asked.

He nodded.

"But that's just superstition."

"That's what I used to think."

"What changed your mind?"

"I joined the Coast Guard."

She just stared at him in silence, waiting for him to say something more—something that made sense.

He fidgeted for a moment and then said, "I've seen a lot of things that have no rational explanation, no matter how hard people try to come up with one. Your husband's boat, for example. There is no reasonable explanation for how it ended up beached on that island a century-and-a-half ago."

He was right. , and if she hadn't seen it with her own eyes, she would have called him crazy or a liar.

"Is there any hope Mark and Dave will make it back?" she asked, her throat constricting.

"I've given up on speculating on things I don't understand. That's one of the reasons I think we should talk to my friend Janis."

"Okay. Set up the meeting."

~

"Land! I see land!" Mark exclaimed excitedly.

"That is the best news I've ever heard," Dave said fervently. "Anything specific?"

"No, I can't make out any structures yet. We must be further

116

up the coast than where we left."

"Maybe," he heard Dave mutter through gritted teeth. Mark ignored the hesitation in Dave's tone.

Fifteen minutes later, Mark was helping the fisherman drag the boat up onto the shore. A short distance away was a town. He could see the steeple of a church towering above everything else, drawing the eye heavenward. He breathed a sigh of relief. Wherever they were, they would soon be home. He couldn't wait to step onto a plane and get back to his wife.

He turned and helped Dave out of the boat as gently as he could. The other man was weak, but at least he was moving, and they'd be able to get him help soon now that they'd reached civilization. The fisherman indicated they should follow him, which they slowly did, given Dave's injuries. As they walked, Mark surveyed their surroundings, trying to figure out where they might be. It was the oddest feeling--it looked like the town that time forgot. He didn't see a single car anywhere on the streets. In fact, everything about it had a bit of an alien feel to him.

The fisherman finally led them into a modest house. A young woman with raven hair, who Mark suspected was the fisherman's daughter, came running when he called. She was beautiful and her eyes immediately gravitated toward Dave. She reached out to him, helping him down into a chair in the front room of the house.

She and her father began conversing rapidly in Spanish. Mark took his phone out of his pocket and turned it on. They hadn't been able to get signal on the island, so he'd left it off to conserve his battery. Now, he'd at last be able to call Sally and let her know he was safe. She must be out of her mind with worry. Tears stung his eyes as he waited for his phone to turn on.

When his home screen came up, he stared in consternation. How could this be?

He still had no signal. He turned slowly in a circle, holding up his phone, hoping against hope to see at least two or three bars.

Nothing.

"No signal?" Dave asked, but unlike Mark, he didn't sound the least bit surprised.

"No. I'll try outside."

"It won't help."

"Why?"

"I recognize the church, even if I don't recognize anything else."

"What?"

Dave indicated the space around them and nodded grimly. "Mark, I don't think we're in Kansas anymore."

"I'm starting to get that, but where the hell are we then?"

Dave shook his head. "Wrong question."

He growled in frustration. "Okay, I'll bite. What's the *right* question?"

"*When* the hell are we?"

"What are you talking about?" Mark asked.

"Look around. No electricity."

Mark took another quick glance around the house. He didn't want to believe it, but it was true. There were hurricane lamps, but no electric lights of any kinds. In fact, there was nothing modern looking anywhere in the house.

The hair on the back of his neck stood on end. There was something very, very wrong here.

"What's going on?" Mark asked.

"I think we're in St. Augustine."

"St. Augustine? This doesn't look anything like St. Augustine."

"Not the St. Augustine you know."

The fisherman and his daughter were still deep in discussion and had moved a little farther away. That was a good thing, because he was about to lose it and he didn't need them watching him throttle his sick friend.

"I need you to be absolutely clear," he said, "before I completely lose it. Tell me what it is you think you know."

"I don't *know* anything."

"Dave, I'm warning you. I need you to tell me what the hell's going on here."

"I think we've somehow traveled through time. I think we're in St. Augustine, but about a couple hundred years ago."

Mark felt as if the bottom was dropping out. His knees grew weak and he staggered to a chair and fell in it. His entire body was shaking uncontrollably.

"It can't be true," he whispered. "Sally."

"I've been to the St. Augustine cathedral. I'm positive that's what we saw on the shore coming in here. The stars aren't right in the sky. For weeks, no one came by the island. The pirates, the lack of cell phone signal even here in a populated town--all of it. It adds up to one thing. All those frightening things that happened to us on the ocean? I think we somehow got thrown back in time."

"This can't be happening," Mark breathed, pressing his fingers to his temples.

Dave called out to their hosts, and in slow, careful Spanish, asked where they were and what year it was. The young woman looked at him as if he'd lost his mind and then said in halting English, "This is St. Augustine. Eighteen-hundred-and-seventy-nine. It is December, sir, six days before *La Misa Del Gallo.*"

"Christmas Eve Mass," Dave said slowly.

Mark dropped his head into his hands and began to sob.

~

Two days later, Sally was a bundle of nerves when she pulled up outside an indie coffee shop. John was just getting out of his car and he waved to her.

"You think your friend will really be able to help?" she asked as she joined him in front of the shop.

"I don't know, but she is an expert in this area. If she can't help, I'm not sure anyone can."

They walked inside, through the shop and then out the back

119

door onto a deck which overlooked the water. It was surprisingly quiet, and only one of the eight tables was occupied. A woman sat with her gaze glued to her laptop, a cup of coffee in her left hand.

She glanced up as they approached, shocking Sally as their eyes met. It was the woman who had been doing the book-signing at Sally's favorite store the day before Mark had disappeared.

"Janis, thanks for meeting us here," John said as they approached.

"Happy to help if I can. Please, have a seat. In truth, you can find me here most days. Writer, coffee shop. I know it's totally cliché, but…there you go." Janis shrugged.

"This has a beautiful view of the ocean," Sally murmured as she took a seat. For some reason, her statement stirred up a wave of anger and betrayal with it. In a way, it was the ocean which had taken away her beloved husband.

"That's why I sit on this side of the table," she said, as if reading Sally's mind. "I never like to turn my back on it. It's better for me always to see what it's up to," Janis said, looking her over.

"Did you lose someone to the ocean?" Sally asked.

"In a fashion. So, John tells me your husband and his friend went missing a few weeks ago?"

Sally nodded.

"Forgive my rudeness, but how do you know he didn't just run off?"

She was not the first person to ask that question, but it still made Sally angry.

"My husband would never have done something like that to me."

"Many husbands do lots of things their wives swear they wouldn't," Janis pointed out.

"Not mine. They were having trouble with their cell phones. The connection was weird and we kept missing each other's calls."

"And I know they got in contact with the Coast Guard because they lost their navigation. Also, one of them, the captain, was injured and needed medical care as quickly as he could get it," John chimed in, his voice tempered but serious. "Two days ago, we found their boat on a remote island. However, it wasn't what we expected at all. This is a picture of it," he said, handing his phone to Janis.

She glanced at it and started to hand it back to him. "Sorry. This must be the wrong picture."

"No, it's not," he said firmly and then cleared his throat.

Her eyebrows shot up in surprise and she pulled the phone back to her, studying the picture in detail.

She paused for a long moment. "Okay, so let's review what you've told me. The two men disappeared mere weeks ago while out fishing. Now you've positively identified their ship. You're telling me that the tree is really growing *through* the boat?"

"Yes," John said jerking his square chin in a firm nod.

"And you're absolutely certain this is the same boat that went missing three weeks ago?"

"One-hundred-percent positive identification," John said.

"I was there. It's my husband's boat," Sally said. "No doubt about it. Only it looks well over a hundred years old and there's no way that can be—which is why we've come to you."

Janis turned to look at her and there was pity in her eyes. "I'm sorry for what I said earlier."

"It's okay. At least you're apologizing for it."

Unlike most of my friends, she thought.

"I must say, this is beyond extraordinary."

"We were hoping you could help us find out what happened with the boat and more importantly, figure out where Mark and Dave might be," John said.

"If you want to find those men, you need to stop looking for them in the here and now," Janis said.

"What do you mean?" Sally asked quickly.

"You need to look for them in the late eighteen-hundreds."

121

17

"It's impossible," Sally said, "what you're suggesting."

Janis waved the phone at her. "You've seen this for yourself and yet you can sit there and say that?"

"Give her some space. It's hard to wrap one's head around," John said, clearly trying to be supportive. "Especially because this is her husband we're talking about."

"So, you're telling us the Bermuda Triangle is like a time machine or portal?" Sally asked.

Janis leaned back in her chair, her demeanor changing as though she were going into some kind of professor lecturing mode. "No one knows with certainty what it is or why it is. However, because of the oddities, it's been studied for many, many years. All we can say for sure is that a disturbing number of ships and planes have gone missing within it."

"If that's true, then how come the government or the Coast Guard doesn't put out warnings about how dangerous the area is?" Sally asked. "Shouldn't people be avoiding it?"

"Yes. They should." Janis sighed. "But despite the evidence, those in the scientific community refuse to acknowledge there is anything unusual going on there. Everyone can point anywhere on the globe to find sudden storms at sea or rogue waves which come up. Dozens of ships sink or get damaged each year because of such violent weather patterns. Some areas are obviously more prone to those than others. People look for the simple explanation--the one that does not challenge their view of the world. They are more concerned with being comfortable with the answer than about being right. So, they ignore things like what happened to your husband and his friend."

"You don't think this was an ordinary storm, then," Sally

said.

Janis shook her head. "There are those, of course, but this...this is something different. Many pilots within the triangle have noticed magnetic anomalies, storms which don't behave like natural storms. They've lost control of their instruments or had them destroyed."

John spoke up. "When your husband and his friend made contact with us, they let us know they had lost their navigation completely."

"Yes, and that has happened to others," Janis said. "Many were lost, but a few were lucky enough to make it back alive. Some have reported strange time anomalies, as if time was standing still."

"Mark and I were texting the night before he disappeared. It was weird because there was a long delay between each text," she said. "And when we tried to talk on the phone, there was just too much distortion and static. It was impossible to hear each other."

"Yes, this has happened to others, as well," Janis said, her voice rising in excitement.

"But what, exactly, are we talking about? What has happened to Mark?"

"There have been many theories about where people end up who disappear in the triangle. It's been postulated that there's a rip in the fabric of this universe and people are slipping through to alternate realities. Others have posited that some sort of alien visitors are taking ships and planes for study or research. However, I have always believed, and I think your husband's case may ultimately help us prove, that it's not a portal to another dimension, but a portal to another time."

"Time travel," Sally murmured.

It seemed fantastical and truly beyond belief. That was what they had all been talking about, dancing around the topic without really saying the words.

"Yes. Time travel. Based on the picture you showed me, I think that the ship, your husband and his friend, were taken

123

back in time."

"Then how do we get them back?" Sally demanded.

"I don't know. This is our first real shot at even proving this is what's happening. I don't have the first clue how to bring them back, but at least we might be able to prove they were there."

"Do you think it's even remotely possible we could bring them back?" Sally asked.

"Yes," John spoke up.

Sally turned to look at him, hope filling her heart for the first time in days.

"Ellen Austin," he murmured with a nod.

"Who's she?" Sally asked.

"Ellen Austin isn't a person. She was a ship that found a boat that disappeared in the triangle in 1881," Janis said, nodding.

"And it came back through time?"

"Yes, before it disappeared again," John said.

Sally felt as if she were on an emotional roller coaster. She was ready to scream and tear her hair out.

"Just tell me what happened to the ship!" she said, realizing she'd raised her voice and was shouting at them in frustration.

"The Ellen Austin was making its run from London to New York," John said. "She came across an abandoned ship in the triangle which was moving at a good clip, but they soon ascertained there was no one on board. The captain of the Ellen Austin sent some of his crew over to the other ship to sail her to New York with them. They boarded her and confirmed there was no sign of the original crew. Then they began sailing together, but shortly thereafter were separated by a freak storm. Two days later they once again found the ship, but the crew the captain had sent over had vanished. He sent over yet another crew, but the ship literally vanished with all hands and this time it didn't reappear."

"So, you think that the ship was slipping back and forth between the two time periods and losing the crew each time in

124

the process?" Janis asked.

"Makes sense to me. I've read some of the reports, and it sounds as if the ship literally disappeared and reappeared before disappearing again. Maybe we should be searching historical records predating 1881 to see if anyone found a ship of that type, or maybe the crew," John said, getting excited.

"I don't think anyone has thought to search in the past for these missing ships and planes before," Janis said, clearly getting equally enthusiastic .

Sally held a hand up. "Even if you find references to these other ships in historic material, how does that help us get Mark and Dave back?"

"I don't know," John said.

"I want Mark *here* with me," Sally groaned. "Not somewhere in the past."

Janis reached across the table and grabbed her hand. "I know how frightening and scary this has to be for you, but at this point, any information we can find is leaps and bounds closer to finding an answer and trying to reverse the process. This is new ground and we're going to have to be patient."

Sally yanked her hand away. "I'm not some academic researcher! This isn't the basis of my next book project. We're talking about my husband! I want him back now!"

"I know how you feel," Janis said.

Sally stood up and slammed her palms against the table. "How could you?" she hissed. "It's not your husband who's lost!"

"No, it's not. I wasn't that lucky. The triangle killed my husband outright," Janis said, raising her voice slightly. "You have a chance at getting yours back, however remote that may be. I would give *anything* for that chance."

Sally stared at her, mouth agape. For the first time since they'd met, she noticed a sadness in Janis' eyes and recognized what it was. It was heartbreak. She knew it because it was what she saw every time she looked in the mirror, how she felt every time she despaired of seeing Mark again. Slowly, she sat down and folded her hands in her lap.

"You lost your husband?" Sally asked quietly.

Janis nodded. "Fourteen years ago. He was a navy pilot. He was sent out on a search and rescue mission when two fighters went missing in the triangle. He found them. Along with their planes. His plane lost instrumentation and all of a sudden they were enveloped in a fog that they described as unnatural. The two fighter pilots were lifers who had been flying forever. In the end, he saved them. He figured out they were all headed in the wrong direction and got them turned around. They were running out of fuel and were barely going to make it to land, but because of my husband, they did."

"What happened to your husband?" Sally whispered, her voice ragged.

"Three minutes before they exited the fog, a bolt of lightning struck his plane and he crashed into the ocean. Both surviving pilots talked to me briefly at the funeral before they were transferred with orders never to speak of what they had seen out there to anyone. The military denied it, of course. They said my husband's death was due to pilot error. They couldn't—or wouldn't--admit the truth. That's all I've ever wanted, you know, is to understand what it was that screwed up the instruments. Was is that fog and why did it take my husband?"

Tears glistened in her eyes and Sally's heart went out to her. "I'm so sorry."

Janis nodded. "It's okay. I've been living with this for a lot longer than you. I want to get closure, understanding for me. But even more than that now, I desperately want to get a happy ending for you."

"Do you think that's even remotely possible?"

Janis nodded. "Yea, I have to believe it is."

Sally reached forward and the two women embraced. When they finally released each other, Sally sat back and wiped her eyes. She glanced at John, who just shook his head.

"I'm not quite as obsessed as Janis with this mystery. I hate

126

losing people to the triangle, but I haven't lost anyone personally."

"That's okay. I'm just grateful you're willing to help," Sally said.

"How can I not?" he asked.

"So, what do we do next?" Sally asked.

Janis leaned forward. "First, I'd like to get a team out to the site of the boat and take some samples, do some scientific dating on it so we can pinpoint exactly when it arrived on that island. Then we'll go from there."

"Okay."

John nodded. "I'll talk to the owner of the island. I'm sure he'll cooperate fully."

"Thank you," Janis said.

"Is it possible Mark and Dave could show up somehow-- somewhere in historical records?" Sally asked.

"I don't know. I think a lot will depend on how long they're trapped there. I mean, we have to believe that they're also doing everything they can wherever and whenever they are to figure out how they can get back here to our time."

~

It had been a week since they had arrived in St. Augustine, and Mark still felt as if he was walking through a dreamscape. At least Dave was on the mend and well on his way to recovery, mostly thanks to the constant care and attention of Rosalyn, the fisherman's daughter, who'd turned out to be something of a genius when it came to herbal medicine.

"I feel like we're in the Twilight Zone," Dave said as he wiped the sweat from his forehead.

Mark grimaced, "Yeah, this is way too weird. No cars, planes, or even Pop Tarts." Mark was on the verge of tears. It was a dumb thing to get upset about, but somehow it had come to represent the whole horror of what they were living through to him.

127

"Dude, lets invent the Pop Tarts and get rich," Dave joked.

"Stop inventing things and just tell me how we're going to find a way back to our own time," Mark said as he wiped the tears from his eyes.

"I don't know. We still don't have any clue how we even got here," Dave countered.

"That storm, or whatever it was, clearly brought us here. We have to assume a similar storm can take us back."

"I think you mean *hope*. We can't assume anything at this point."

"Come on," Mark said, frustration filling him. "You're the one who's always talking about having faith. Don't let me down now."

"I'm sorry. I'm just barely crawling out of the grave. That alone feels like a massive miracle to me and it's hard to wrap my head around anything else at this point."

"Well, wrap your head around this. We're going home. I don't care what it takes or how long it takes, but we will get there. We have to."

Dave chuckled. "When we do, this will make one heck of a story. We'll be famous."

"That's right! Now you've got the proper attitude."

"The only question is, which one of us is going to write it?"

"You're the educated one, I'll leave it to you," Mark said. "I just want to go home to my wife."

Dave chuckled, "Says the man with a couple of Ph.D.'s."

"You know me. I don't like to write."

"It is a lost art."

"There, sorted. You'll write our heroic story of survival and time travel and all of it. I'll go home to my family where I belong."

"Sounds like a plan," Dave said, actually smiling.

"There, that looks like the old Dave I know. You were really starting to worry me."

"*I* was starting to worry me," his friend admitted.

"We still have to figure out what to do. Sailing *The*

Guardians is out of the question, especially given everything else. There's no way we can repair it," Mark said. "That hull is toast."

"Agreed."

"So, we need to get our hands on another boat and get back out there on the ocean. We need to track down the fog and the storm that brought us here so we can get back to our time."

"You know, it's possible that even if we encounter the same anomaly, and that's highly unlikely, it won't take us to the future as we want but will send us further back into the past."

"I'm trying not to think about that," Mark admitted.

~

Sally woke up and out of habit reached for Mark. Her searching fingers only found his pillow, though. She sat up slowly, trying to clear the cobwebs from her head. She reached for her phone and froze when she saw the date.

It was their wedding anniversary and Mark was not there.

"Happy Anniversary, Baby. I'll see you soon," she whispered out loud.

She got up, showered and got dressed. She went into the kitchen and set about figuring out her day. In a few moments she would wake up the girls and get breakfast started.

As she sat sipping a cup of coffee, she tried to organize her thoughts. The doorbell rang and she went to see who it could possibly be so early in the morning.

She opened the door and was startled when a young man thrust a massive bouquet of purple tulips at her. Before she could say anything, he was gone. She closed the door and slowly walked into the kitchen, her heart in her throat. Mark always gave her purple tulips on their anniversary, as it had been their wedding color. She wondered where these had come from.

She put the bouquet down on the kitchen counter and found the card. Her heart leapt into her throat as she read it.

For my darling wife, Happy Anniversary. Forever yours, Mark.

18

Sally's hand froze as she stared at the card. It was typewritten, so she couldn't see her husband's handwriting, but there was his name as clear as day. Purple tulips were their flower. He had given them to her on their first date. She'd carried them at their wedding. He'd given them to her every anniversary since then.

She looked at the name of the florist, Petal Perfect. It sounded familiar to her for some reason. She grabbed her phone and called them.

"Good morning, Petal Perfect," an older gentleman said when he answered the phone.

"Hello. This is Sally White. I just received some purple tulips."

"Yes, Mrs. White, Happy Anniversary. Was there something wrong with the flowers?" he asked.

"No, they're lovely, thank you. But the card says that they're from my husband."

"Of course. Mr. White prepays every year for the next year's bouquet. He jokes that it's so that he can never forget your anniversary. Trust me, though, that's one husband who would never forget, no matter what. He's head over heels for you. You've got a good one there."

"So what you're saying is he paid for these last year?"

"Yes."

"I see," she said, her heart dropping in disappointment. It was ridiculous, but for a moment she had let herself hope he'd somehow made it back somewhere and had sent the flowers before calling—or better yet, showing up at home. He wouldn't have done that, of course, but she was grasping at every straw she could.

"Is something wrong?" the older man asked, his voice kind.

"Mark's boat was…lost at sea…a few weeks ago," she said, struggling to get the words out. "I just thought…"

"Oh, Mrs. White, I'm so sorry. He was a wonderful man," he said, sounding shocked and saddened.

"Thank you."

"If there's anything I can do…" he said, letting his words trail off.

She was touched at the show of kindness from a stranger. Then again, it sounded as if he'd had at least some dealings with Mark for the past few years. She took a deep breath. She was only now beginning to understand how many lives Mark had touched. He'd been such a special man.

No. He *is* such a special man. She could not—would not—give up.

"That is very kind of you. I really do appreciate the flowers," she said. "It was just startling."

"I can imagine. I remember the first time I met your husband. He couldn't have been more than fourteen or so. One day he came into my shop all excited and nervous. He told me he was looking for flowers for a very special girl. Naturally, I suggested roses. He said that everyone did that and that he wanted something special, something which would make it look as if he'd put a lot of thought into it. He told me they were finally going on their first real date and she was a princess. He was drawn to the tulips and I suggested purple, the color of royalty, since he'd said she was a princess. He seemed so happy when he'd decided on them. A few years later, he showed me the engagement ring he'd selected for her when he came in to order more purple tulips. I can tell you that he has always loved you and that it has always warmed my heart to see just how devoted he was to you."

"That means so much to me," she said. "Thank you for sharing that with me."

"It's the least I can do. And I know if there is any way on

this earth, he will find his way home to you."

"I hope so," she said, wondering why he would say such a thing.

"Please, do let me know if you hear anything. Mark was more than just a customer. I considered him a friend."

"I will," she promised.

She finally hung up the phone and her heart was full. She felt like crying, but instead, she made herself smile as she pressed the tulips to her face and inhaled deeply. Wherever he was, Mark was still looking out for her, thinking about her. She could tangibly feel it as she stood there holding the flowers he had sent her.

Flowers from the past.

It was ironic, but at the same time terribly poetic.

After a minute, she got a vase out of a cabinet, filled it with water and carefully arranged the tulips in it. They were the most beautiful tulips she had ever seen. As she stared at them, she could feel Mark's love wrapping around her, warming her heart.

She smiled.

"Happy Anniversary, Mark," she whispered again, this time with hope in her heart.

~

Mark had been struggling to keep track of the number of days they'd been gone. As far as he could tell, they had been thrown back a hundred and forty years and in a different month altogether from the one in which they'd left. By his calculations, though, back home it was their wedding anniversary.

Which made it fitting that today was their first attempt to make it home.

He and Dave had managed to requisition a small, rickety fishing boat. The thing was barely seaworthy and was far more likely to kill them than transport them into the future. Still, it was a start, and it was with unswerving hope in his heart that he boarded it, clutching in his fist some purple wildflowers he had found.

They were a gift for Sally, should they make it back to her time. He hadn't been able to find any tulips, so it was the best he could do.

"What do you think?" he asked Dave as he began to row out into the ocean. The small ship had a mast and sail they could use to direct the boat once they got a bit farther from shore.

"I don't know," Dave said. "The locals seemed to think the next three days would be a bad time to be on the water. They warned us against sailing out into it. That we'd be putting ourselves in danger—which we probably are. I didn't entirely understand the superstition, but for our purposes, we need to find a strange, unexplainable storm. Hopefully that's what we're sailing toward."

"Hopefully," Mark agreed. "How's the foot?"

"It hurts like the dickens. I wouldn't wish this on my worst enemy, but at least I can put some weight on it now, which is an improvement."

Mark chuckled.

"What's so funny?"

"The thought of you having an enemy. You're Mr. Nice Guy, and a priest, to boot."

"Hey, you weren't there in seminary. Joey Moretti and I got into a fistfight."

"A fistfight. In *seminary*? Uh huh. Right. Over what?"

"Whether or not free will has an impact on our lives."

Mark rolled his eyes and continued to row. Of course, he had gotten into a fight about theology.

Only Dave.

What they were doing was dangerous. Both of them knew it, but neither wanted to say it out loud. The boat was not in the greatest shape, but it was the best they'd been able to borrow for their venture given their time limitations, in both senses of the word. No one in their right mind would want to sail it into a storm, especially the kind for which they were looking.

He was in his right mind but in the wrong century and he couldn't sit idly by and let his life run out here. He needed to be back with his family. His wife and children needed him and he needed them. He wouldn't rest until he walked back into the door of his home.

Even if they survived the coming storm, they still might end up hopelessly lost at sea, either in this time or another, and die of starvation and thirst before they ever made it home. Both of them were carrying compasses with them which hopefully would not betray them as their electronic navigation equipment had.

He had finally rowed far enough away from shore that they were able to unfurl the small sail. The boat began moving at a brisk pace farther out to sea.

"Here we go. You ready?" Dave asked, excitement in his voice.

Mark spoke through a clenched jaw. "Ready to go home. I don't think anyone can be ready for what it will take us to get there."

It seemed like it forever, but they finally made it out to roughly the area in which they figured they had been when the original storm had taken them back in time.

The skies in the distance were dark when they finally hauled down the sail. Could this be the storm they were awaiting?

Both of them were wearing jackets made out of cork, the closest thing to a life vest they could come by in the 1800's. Mark would have liked to have taken a couple of more modern vests from his boat, but that meant going out of their way and risking running aground on the island again, which neither one of them was willing to do. Even thinking about it caused both of them anxiety.

"Well, here we are," Dave said with a deep sigh.

"Yeah. Here we are," Mark echoed. "Think there's any chance this will work?"

"I wish I knew."

They fell into a tense silence as both of them kept their eyes glued on the dark clouds moving steadily closer to their rickety boat. Even as the skies grew angrier, the ocean grew still. It was an odd, bipolar combination as electricity went through the air.

Hold on, Baby, I'm coming, he kept thinking, willing Sally to hear him through time and distance.

~

Just as she was about to wake the girls up for breakfast, Sally froze with her hand on the doorknob of their bedroom door. She could have sworn she'd heard Mark's voice calling out to her.

"Mark?" she whispered, her heart thudding in response. "Is that you?"

~

"Sally?" Mark asked aloud.

"What?" Dave said, cocking his head in surprise.

Mark shook his head. "It was the strangest thing. I could have sworn I heard Sally's voice for a moment. Too much stress, I guess."

Dave raised an eyebrow. "Something like that ever happen to you before?"

"I'm not crazy, if that's what you're asking."

"No. That's not what I'm saying. I mean, do you guys ever communicate without actually talking?"

Mark hesitated for a moment. "When Sally was pregnant with Emma, I once heard her tell me clear as day that she was frightened about what it was going to mean for our relationship. She was at home at the time and I was at work. It freaked me out so much I went straight home to tell her I loved her, that she was and would always be my number one and nothing could ever change that. She told me later that she'd been rehearsing what she wanted to say to me when I got home that evening and somehow I had heard her word-for-word."

136

"Wow."

"Yeah. Then when she was pregnant with Jayne, I'm positive I heard her several times—heart-to-heart. And she heard me, too. It mostly seemed to happen when one or both of us was experiencing intense emotions."

"What kind of emotions?"

"All kinds. Happy, sad, angry, even crazy hungry a couple of times."

"So, do you think this might be one of those times?"

He shook his head. "I don't know. It stopped when Jayne was born and we haven't really had any of those experiences since."

"I can't even begin to understand what it would mean to have that kind of connection with another human being," Dave said.

"You believe me?" Mark asked, surprised by his friend's reaction.

"Believing in the miraculous kind of goes with the job, you know."

Mark chuckled. "Yeah, I guess so."

"I'm guessing both of you are highly emotional right now and have been for weeks. That's only natural. You've both been under tremendous strain such as most people could never imagine."

"Yeah, but this is the first time it's happened," Mark said.

"Odd. I wonder what triggered it now?" Dave mused.

"I've been carefully keeping track of the days we've been gone. Today is our wedding anniversary."

"Oh, man, I'm so sorry. No wonder you're full of pent-up emotion."

"Yeah, well get me home safe and sound and you won't ever have to get us an anniversary gift, not even for our fiftieth."

"Sounds like a plan."

They fell silent again as both of them returned their attention to the approaching storm.

137

Watching, waiting and hoping.

~

Sally stood frozen for a moment, straining her ears and her heart to listen, but she didn't hear anything else.

Suddenly, a wave of nausea washed over her. She let go of the doorknob and ran for the bathroom down the hall. As she knelt in front of the toilet, she closed her eyes, trying to wish the sickness away.

Mark, I wish you were here, she thought in misery. *I can't do this again, not without you.*

Again.

The word rang through her mind, echoing around and around.

Again.

There was something her subconscious had known which she hadn't yet fully grasped. Despite her best efforts, she couldn't calm her stomach and she began to throw up. As she did her thoughts were racing back to the last time she'd been sick like this.

She'd been pregnant with Jayne.

This time, the clues had all been there, but she'd been so wrapped up in her search for Mark she'd missed them.

I'm pregnant.

19

Her nausea was overwhelming, causing Sally's head to spin as her mind struggled to come to terms with what was happening.

I can't be pregnant. Not now. Not with Mark trapped in the past. I can't do this alone.

Even while her mind was busy denying the truth, her body was making it emphatically clear. She would take a pregnancy test, but she instinctively knew even without confirmation. She could feel it, just as she had with her last two pregnancies.

She and Mark had talked about having a third child, but they had never made a decision to try to get pregnant. It looked as if nature had made the choice for them. She kept her eyes squeezed tightly closed against the dizzying motion of the room spinning around her.

"Mama, are you okay?" Emma asked from behind her, her voice high and frightened.

Sally raised her left arm and gave her a thumbs up since she couldn't speak at the moment. Emma ran from the room, her bare feet slapping against the floor. "Just a minute, Mama."

At long last, the waves of nausea ended. She was finally able to stand up and wash her hands and splash cold water on her face. She turned around as she heard bare feet running back toward the bathroom.

Emma came through the door holding a box of Saltine crackers, which she thrust forward with a worried expression on her face.

"This is what you give me when I'm sick," she said.

"Thank you, sweetheart. That's very thoughtful of you. Mama's not sick, though."

"Then what's wrong with you? I heard you throwing up."

"Mama's growing a baby in her belly."

Emma squealed in delight and clapped her hands together. "Baby brother?"

"Maybe. I don't know yet. It may be a baby sister."

"I think it will be a boy," Emma said firmly. "I was going to ask Santa for a baby brother but I guess he already knew."

Despite all the angst and melancholy her discovery had left her, Sally couldn't help but smile softly at Emma's determination. She reached out and grabbed her daughter and gave her a bear hug, then kissed the top of her head.

Her children were so dear to her. This new baby would be, as well, no matter what the future held for them.

"Mama loves you so much," she whispered.

"I love you, too, Mama."

"How about we have ice cream and fried pickles for breakfast?"

Emma wrinkled up her nose. "Can we have regular pickles and fried ice cream instead?"

Sally laughed. It was the first time she had done so since Mark had disappeared and the sound surprised her. She pressed one hand to her still-flat abdomen and put the other on Emma's head.

Where there's life, there's hope, she thought.

She heard another set of footsteps coming down the hall. Jayne appeared, rubbing her eyes sleepily.

"What's going on?" she asked.

"We're getting a baby brother!" Emma squealed.

"Or sister," Sally warned, even though she knew Emma wasn't listening.

"I want a little brother! Brother! Brother!" Jayne chanted.

"We don't get a choice. We have to be happy with whichever one we get," Sally explained.

"Why don't we get to choose?" Jayne asked.

"Father Dave would say it's because God chooses for us and knows what's best for our family."

Their eyes went round at that explanation and their mouths formed little O's.

Emma turned to Jayne and said solemnly, "We both need to ask Santa for a brother because he and God are friends. And Daddy says that friends do things for each other."

Sally bit her lip. Such an innocent statement, and yet it pierced her heart as sharply as a dagger. She hoped that wherever they were—*whenever* they were-- Mark and Dave were taking care of each other.

"When can we go see Santa?" Emma asked, turning back to her.

"Not for a few more weeks yet. It's not quite time for Christmas. We'll go and talk to him after Thanksgiving."

"Won't it be too late then?" Emma asked, her eyes widening.

"No, honey. It won't be. The baby won't be here until next summer."

"He's a slowpoke," Jayne said. "Tell him to hurry up."

"Daddy's going to have to come home now," Emma said. "He has to be here for the baby."

Sally sucked in her breath as if she'd been punched in the gut. "He'll get home just as soon as he can," she said.

"Who's going to help you until he gets here?"

"Well, you two are going to be big sisters, so you can be Mama's helpers," she said.

Both girls stood up a little straighter, looking excited and proud.

"I'll be the best helper ever," Emma said.

"No, I will be," Jayne contradicted her.

Sally smiled at each of them. "Tell you what. The first one to the kitchen gets to help me make breakfast."

They both turned and ran from the room as fast as they could, squealing in delight all the way. She smiled even as tears filled her eyes. The next several months were going to be rougher than she could have ever imagined.

~

Mark's hands were clenched in fists as the wind buffeted the boat. They had reached the vanguard of the storm, coming at them with such a sudden ferocity it nearly knocked the breath out of him. The wind whistled around them and the boat creaked and groaned in response, creating a chorus of sound which sent shivers down his spine.

Things were about to get brutal. He glanced at Dave. The priest's face was pale and he was scowling. A vein in his throat was pulsing rapidly.

He thought of all the people in town who had declared it sheer suicide to be on the water during the upcoming storm.

Maybe they were right, but he had to try to get home, no matter what it took.

"I'm sorry I got you into this mess," he said.

"None of this is on you," Dave said tersely.

"Still, I'm sorry. I also want you to know that I trust you completely and there's no one I'd rather have face hell with me than you."

"Really?" Dave asked, turning to look at him.

"Absolutely. You're a rock. I know I can count on you to do the right thing, make the best choice in any situation, no matter what."

"Well, that's not ominous sounding." A half-smile tugged at Dave's lips.

"I guess I'm trying to say, don't let me get us both killed," Mark said.

"It's not just you. I want to get home as badly as you do."

"Yeah, but you're not likely to do something stupid trying to get us there."

"I don't know about that. Waiting like sitting ducks for this storm to hit us feels pretty stupid to me at the moment."

I know what you mean, Mark thought. The closer the storm got, the more he suspected they were making a mistake. There were too many variables. It all felt wrong.

"I keep waiting for everything to go dark or for the crazy fog to roll in," Dave muttered.

Mark nodded. That's what it was. They had far too much visibility. It felt like a normal storm, even if it was going to be a monster. The waves which were now racing to catch the wind were violent, but they were just waves. There was nothing supernatural-looking or feeling about them.

"Do you get the feeling this isn't the storm we're looking for?" he finally asked.

"More with every passing second," Dave admitted.

"Great. So we're out in the middle of a massive storm that's not even going to take us back home. What are we supposed to do now?"

"We hold on like crazy--because it's here!"

The sky opened up above them and dumped so much water down that in moments, Mark was gasping for breath because it felt as if he was being drowned. There was so much water that it grayed out his sight. He couldn't even see Dave anymore. The boat suddenly crested a wave then just as suddenly dropped with a bang. The blow jerked him completely off balance and he purposely fell down onto the deck before he slipped and found himself flying over the side and being consumed by the angry gray waves surrounding them. He prayed that Dave had done the same.

He hugged the deck, tucking his head so he could breathe.

We're going to die! he thought, his oxygen-starved brain panicking as he sucked air into his lungs and then began to cough out water.

It can't end like this, he thought. This couldn't be the end for Sally and him, for their love story. *Our love is bigger than storms and time and death. Nothing will keep me from her.*

The small boat bucked up and down and he continued to cling to the deck, breathing when he could and holding his breath the rest of the time as water dashed over him. He closed his eyes against the pounding of the rain and surf.

He pictured Sally in his mind, getting a crystal clear vision of her. He clung to the memory of the first time they'd gone out on the water together. The sun had been bright and high in the sky, beaming down on them. Its rays had hit her hair and reflected on it until it seemed as if it was glowing, as if she was some kind of angel.

My angel.

He could practically hear her laughter, light and lovely and ringing so clearly in his mind that it drowned out the sounds of the storm. When she laughed, she wasn't shy or restrained. She would throw her head back and give herself over to the joy of the moment.

He had always loved that about her.

He managed to take another breath, and instead of salty sea air, he imagined he was breathing in her scent. It was a heady, rich, intoxicating mix of vanilla and cinnamon. For years he had thought it must be the soap or shampoo she used. He only knew the fragrance drove him wild. After they had married, he had discovered the scent was all her own.

He let the storm fade away in his mind as he fixed his thoughts entirely on Sally. Every detail about her. It calmed him down and his breathing grew steadier and more even.

She is the only compass I need.

Suddenly, in his heart, he knew he would return to her. But not today. Not for a long time, he feared.

It would take tremendous blood and toil and heartache, but he *would* return to her.

A terrible roaring, cracking sound tore his focus away from Sally. He glanced up to see the mast bearing down on him. He shouted in dismay, but there wasn't time to move out of the way before it struck him hard. He went flying and a moment later his body hit the water. Everything went black.

20

Though she didn't eat very much, Sally had managed to make it through most of breakfast without running back to the bathroom again. She decided if she could finish eating and get everything cleaned up without having to vomit again, it was a victory.

She watched Emma and Jayne as they ate. Both girls were giggling and talking excitedly about who they hoped was going to be their baby brother. They were so sweet, so innocent. She wished they could stay that way forever.

She would give anything to protect them from the harsh realities of life. That's why she still hadn't told them about their father.

What could she say? She couldn't tell them the truth. Even if they could understand a concept beyond most adult's comprehension, they weren't yet old enough to be trusted to keep a secret. If they accidently told other people what had happened to their father, it would quickly get ugly and probably dangerous. People would call her crazy and possibly try to take her children away from her.

As it was, people were getting edgier and edgier about the fact that she continued to refuse to hold a funeral. She supposed she wasn't surprised that no one understood why she was holding out, especially because she couldn't tell anyone the whole truth. But she knew it was only a matter of time before someone said something to the girls, either by accident or on purpose.

She wasn't yet prepared for that day to come.

She might never be.

Her phone rang, startling her out of her reverie. She grabbed it off the counter and glanced at the Caller ID.

It was Janis.

"Hello?" she asked, her breath catching in her throat.

"Hi, how are you doing?"

"Okay. Did you…" she glanced at the girls and walked slowly to the living room, cupping the phone with her other hand and speaking in a soft tone. "What did you find?"

"We took samples from the boat, the soil, the trees growing through it--all of it. Everything we could. I wanted to call you right away because the results have come back."

"And?"

"As near as they can tell, the boat has been there since the 1860s."

Her chest tightened and she suddenly couldn't breathe. Even though she'd been prepared for this answer, it still gutted her. "One hundred and seventy years."

"Yeah."

Her stomach twisted hard. "I'll call you back."

She ended the call and ran for the bathroom.

~

Mark awoke with a start as salt water splashed against his lips and flooded his mouth. He coughed. His lungs felt as if they were on fire. His head was spinning and part of him wanted to return to the darkness.

Another wave splashed him.

I'm in the water, he realized, panic racing through him. He started to kick and splash out with his arms, twisting around as he looked for the boat.

"Stop fighting me!" Dave yelled.

Only then did Mark realize the priest had his arm clamped around his chest. He immediately stopped kicking and lifted his chin for a breath.

"What happened?"

"The mast cracked. It hit you hard and knocked you into the

146

water. I dove in after you and the whole ship went down seconds later."

"How long was I out?" Mark asked, realizing the wind and rain had diminished to almost nothing. That mast must have hit him hard enough to completely knock him out for quite some time.

Dave's breathing was ragged. "It felt like forever. Probably about an hour."

"You've been keeping me afloat for an hour?" he asked, shocked beyond comprehension.

"No. Thankfully, the cork jacket took care of that, for the most part. I've been keeping you from flipping over so that your face was submerged. Making sure you were floating on your back and not taking in too much water. The cork jacket would have been useless to me if you still drowned."

"Oh, man. I'm so sorry."

"Stop saying that," Dave said. "You apologize about everything, and none of this is on you. You think you can keep yourself upright now? I could use a break."

"Yeah."

Dave moved his arm a bit and after a moment, let go. Mark began to tilt forward and he stretched out his arms to right himself.

"So, on a scale of one to ten, how screwed are we?" Mark asked.

"Well, you know. I'm just guessing here, but it's only about…ten."

"Great. As long as we're not in too much trouble."

"Yeah, it's cool. We've got several minutes left before we die hideous deaths."

"Well, as long as we're not too rushed. You know, I've got a whole laundry list of things I need to say to you."

"Remember, I know you. I'm not sure we have long enough for you to actually confess your sins."

"Please. I'm a saint and you know it."

"Right. I always forget that part. I'll have to remember to

147

notify the Pope about you if we live through this," Dave said.

"Yeah, you get right on that."

"I will--just as soon as you figure out a way to get us back alive. You know, not only to land, but also to the future?"

"You've had an entire hour out here without interruptions to think about it and you haven't solved the world's problems yet?" Mark asked.

"The world's yes. Ours, not so much. I had to leave something for you to do when you woke up."

"Great. Thanks for that."

"Hey, what are friends for?" Dave said. He smirked.

Mark stared at him wide-eyed. For a moment he imagined Dave was on the verge of completely losing it. They were out in the middle of the ocean about to drown and Dave was grinning like a cat.

Mark suddenly felt the corners of his own mouth twitching and before he knew it, he was laughing, too.

If he's going crazy, then it's catching.

They laughed together for a minute, the laughter of men who were glad, if surprised, to still be alive, for however long that was going to be.

"How about we figure out a way to get back onto land and into some dry clothes?" Dave finally said. "It's freezing out here."

"Now you're speaking my language."

At that moment, they heard a ship's bell ringing in the distance. Mark twisted around. There, in the distance, was the same exact fishing boat which had rescued them last time. He put his fingers to his lips and responded with a loud whistle. Then he and Dave both began shouting and waving their arms. The boat bore down on them, and ten minutes later they were sitting on its deck, wrapped in warm blankets.

The fisherman had looked less than pleased to see them again and had grumbled a lot under his breath.

Loco was the only word Mark had understood.

"We're lucky he came out here," Mark said.

Despite the cold, Dave turned red. "It was a little more than luck."

"What?"

"Apparently his daughter was worried about--um, me." He cleared his throat. "She forced him to come after us."

Mark grinned and slapped Dave on the shoulder. "Look at you, impressing the beautiful ladies."

"That's so not funny," Dave said, turning even redder, if that were possible.

"Oh yes, it really is."

"Knock it off."

"Look, just tell her the truth. You're a Catholic priest. Married to the Church and all that."

"But I'm not," Dave pointed out.

"Um, last I checked, you were," Mark said, raising an eyebrow.

"Not here. Not now. There's no way for me to prove it. I have no papers. No bishop in this time period knows anything about me, and I don't want to draw attention to the fact that I know almost nothing about this time period and its customs."

"I thought things in the Church have pretty much stayed the same for two thousand years."

"Yes, but there are some subtleties, nuances… Look, the last thing either of us needs is to be accused of being heretics. Or worse."

Mark stared at him for a minute before asking, "You're afraid that if you try to be a priest here you'll screw up in some way you couldn't have anticipated and you'll end up being excommunicated?"

"Yes."

"But, does that count? It's not even your time period. I mean, does someone from the past have authority over you instead of your own superiors in the future?"

"I've been going over and over it in my mind, and all I know is that I really don't want to find out. Like I told you—I want to go home as badly as you do. So, I can't be a priest here."

"Okay. Kiss the girl, then," Mark teased.

"I'm still a priest!"

"But not here."

"I made a vow to God."

Mark could see his friend's dilemma, but to him, it didn't seem like the most pressing of their concerns at that moment. "Well, let's focus on getting back to our time before it becomes too much of an issue."

"I'm all for that, but that's become even more problematic."

"How so?"

"Do you think anyone else is going to lend us a boat after what we've just pulled?" Dave asked.

"Then we'll have to buy our own."

"With what?"

"I don't know. We have the advantage of having come from the future, don't we? I was hoping you'd have an idea about how we can make a whole lot of money in 1880 Florida."

Dave started to shake his head but then stopped. His eyes lit up. "I don't know *how* to make a lot of money, but I know where we can *find* a lot of money."

"Okay, where? And please don't tell me we're going to rob a bank. I know that desperate times call for desperate measures and all that, but I don't think I could be a part of that."

"Not a bank. The Lita del Alma."

Mark stared at him. "What is that?"

"It's a Spanish treasure ship that sunk off the coast of Florida."

"Like the Atocha?"

"Yeah. It's one of just dozens of wrecks off the coast."

"I'm not familiar with it."

"You wouldn't be unless you've read some of the more obscure books on Floridian history. It went down in 1759 and was found in the late 1890s by a man named John Lundy. He was the great-great-great grandson of one of three survivors who were in a rowboat heading for land when the ship went

150

down. He spent nearly two decades searching for it."

"Why did it take that long?"

"It was dark and the men came to shore quite a distance south. The location was passed down in the family, but the sailor was never completely certain exactly where the ship went down."

"How does that help us? I mean, he was a sailor on the ship and it took him twenty years to find it. I don't have that kind of time, especially if we're racing against him."

"We have one advantage," Dave said.

"Which would be what?"

"I know where it is."

21

"What do you mean you know where it is?" Mark asked, bewildered.

"One of my friends with whom I served in the Navy was Lundy's great grandson. He took me out a few times to see what was left of the wreck. I know exactly where it is. We might have to compensate some for the tidal drift, since it's more than a hundred years earlier, but basically, we've got ourselves sunken treasure," he said excitedly.

Mark didn't want to burst his friend's bubble, but he felt he had to douse the fire with more realistic expectations. "But we have no equipment that can make it down there. Scuba diving isn't a thing yet."

"They do have weight belts and I think we have scuba gear on the Guardians. The Lita del Alma went down in a little less than thirty feet of water. There are free divers who can go deeper than that."

"Okay, but even if we can find it and reach it, what does that do for us regarding the future? Not to mention how it will affect other people. I mean, if the treasure isn't there for John Lundy to find, then you'll never hear about it in the future to know about it now when you come back to the past. Isn't that how time travel works? A big loop?"

"I haven't a clue how time travel actually works. I'm not a nuclear physicist, I'm a priest. What I *do* know is that the sterncastle of the Lita del Alma, where a lot of the wealth was supposedly kept, is still missing. Maybe we *are* meant to find it. Maybe we always found it, and that's why no one else does in the future."

"This is insane. You are frying my brain here. Anyway, it

will take forever to dive for treasure like that. *And* we'd still have to get somebody to loan us a boat so we could search for the treasure, which, as we've already covered, is highly unlikely after today. I want to get home *now*, not years from now," Mark said, his voice raspy with frustration.

Dave put a hand on his shoulder. "We both want to get home. Until we can, we need funds in the here and now. We don't know how long it's going to take us to find the perfect storm or the right conditions or whatever it was that caused us to time travel back in the first place. After seeing what happened today, we have to be prepared to go out over and over, and that's going to cost money, especially if we keep losing ships in the process."

Mark took a deep breath. "You're right. I don't like it, but you're right."

"I'm always right."

"Okay. I guess we're about to Indiana Jones the heck out of this thing."

~

Sally walked into the coffee shop, ready to have another meeting with Janis. After finishing breakfast, she'd dropped the girls off at her parents' house. She'd called Janis back and the other woman had agreed to meet with her.

Janis was at her usual table out on the back deck with a large stack of books sitting next to her on the table. When Sally slid into the chair across from her, Janis reached out and squeezed her hand.

"How are you holding up?" Janis asked.

"I've been better, but I'm glad to know something, even if it is bizarre."

"I can imagine. I want you to know that I'm going to do everything I can to help you figure out a way to get him back."

"I appreciate that."

"I've brought you some books I thought you might want to

153

read. I believe it's important that we research not only the triangle itself, but also the time period in which they ended up."

"Why?"

"We may be able to figure out if there's an explanation, some type of magnetic force or other anomalies which were known to occur in that time period. Maybe we can figure out why the triangle sent them there, or *then*, rather, instead of some other time."

"So, you don't think they were dumped into a random time period?"

"No, I don't. I have nothing to back up that theory, but we are truly in uncharted territory here. The more we can learn, the better chance we have to figure all of this out."

"Okay, I can buy that," Sally said with a nod.

"Good. On the plus side, there are some rather interesting events and some very detailed accounts of 1880s Florida, particularly by Lawrence Whitcomb."

"Who was he?"

"He was a theologian and philosopher who arrived in St. Augustine around 1880. He wrote extensively about the time, the people. His writings are considered rather groundbreaking and don't conform to a lot of the writing conventions of the time. He had a great deal of compassion for people."

"Okay," Sally said. The name rang a bell, but she didn't think she'd ever read any of his writings. "Are there any similarities about the disappearances in the triangle?"

"Yes and no," Janis said. "The ships and planes that have disappeared are of all types and sizes. There are disappearances during every time of year and day of the week. As far as I know, no researcher has ever found any kind of pattern as far as the time of day or year or type of craft."

"Okay, so it's all totally random."

"Apparently. If there is a commonality of some sort, no one has yet found it."

"So where do the similarities come into play?" Sally asked. "Or are there any that you know of?"

"Loss of radio communication, usually quite sudden. Some crafts that disappear report everything is normal, that they are on schedule, and then suddenly they just vanish. There are some who have escaped the triangle and reported strange phenomenon while inside--specifically, interruption in communication, navigation anomalies and compasses going crazy as if there is some kind of magnetic interference. Some have reported sudden storms or strange, intense fog that comes out of nowhere. Others have reported mental disorientation, no matter how experienced the pilot is."

"I know Mark and Dave lost their instruments and encountered some kind of heavy fog," Sally said.

Janis nodded. "I'm not surprised to hear that."

"Communication was also strange. I'm not sure about the ship's instruments, but Mark and I kept getting static when we tried to call each other on our cell phones. He left me a message that arrived a day later, and when we were texting, there was a very long lag time between messages."

"As if communication was somehow being disrupted," Janis mused.

"Or as if time was in flux," Sally pointed out.

"You could be right about that. It makes sense, in a way."

"And no one can anticipate these fogs or magnetic disturbances?"

"No," Janis said. "The oceans are always unpredictable on the best of days, but whatever happens in the triangle defies logic or reason. Every year, ships are sunk all over the world, but few vanish entirely. Now, thanks to your husband, we have new information as to why they are vanishing."

"Mark always liked to push the boundaries and try new things in his work. Why not in this," Sally said with a groan. The thought made her sad, but also in a small way amused her. How very Mark, always the pioneer in everything.

"Do you think we might be able to find historical records of them?" she asked.

"I think we should try. If they are in the past, it's possible

155

they might try to find a way to communicate with us. That is, if it occurs to them that we'll even be looking. I've already done a cursory search and haven't found anything that jumped out at me. That's another area where you'll be a huge help. You'll probably have a lot more luck recognizing their fingerprints than I ever would."

"Sure, I can do that," Sally said. She couldn't help the tiny spark of hope that lit within her, that maybe Mark had somehow tried to communicate with her.

"Divide and conquer," Janis said with a tight smile. "These books are yours to get started with."

"Looks like I have a lot of reading to do," Sally said as she sized up the stack.

She didn't care if she had to read a million books or spend thousands of hours online if it meant bringing Mark home.

~

After three days of rest, Mark was itching to get back onto the water. It felt as if every day spent on land was one day with Sally lost forever. His desperation was growing by the minute. Dave was right, though. In order to continue trying to find a way to make it home, they needed their own boat--and they weren't going to get that without money.

As it turned out, Rosalyn spoke limited English, and she helped them explain to her father that they wanted to find sunken treasure. He called them *loco* several times, and Mark couldn't blame him for questioning their sanity, but in the end, his daughter was persuasive. Mark was beginning to think she could talk anybody into anything.

After all, it was clear to him that the young woman had set her eyes on David. It was equally clear that she had succeeded in getting under his skin and that despite his vows, Dave was falling for her.

So together, the four of them planned their first expedition to try and recover some of the treasure from the Lita del Alma.

~

Sally had spent three days reading everything Janis had given her about the Bermuda Triangle. The more she read, the angrier she grew that there hadn't been a concerted effort to solve the mystery of the triangle, or to at least try to protect and warn travelers in its path.

Finished with that chore, she turned to the stack of books relating to the history of Florida in the 1880s. She grabbed the first book, entitled *Culture and Myth*. Before she could open it, the author's name jumped out at her.

D. Lawrence Whitcomb.

Janis had mentioned Lawrence, but she hadn't said it was the author's middle name. Now, staring at the name a chill ran down her spine. She knew that name. Lawrence was Dave's middle name. Whitcomb was his mother's maiden name. He had gone by D. Lawrence Whitcomb on more than one occasion during his college years when he and Mark were up to some prank or some other time when he was trying not be recognized.

Sally opened the book with shaking hands. There was a dedication inside.

To Mark, my best friend through tribulations no man should ever have to suffer. May your voyages take you to where you belong. And to his lovely wife, Sally, I pray you keep hope and faith alive no matter how bleak things might appear. In the end, love really does conquer all.

She pressed the book to her heart as tears blurred her vision. Mark was trying to come home to her and Dave was urging her to not give up.

She wouldn't.

With her dying breath, she'd be waiting, expecting Mark's arrival.

22

The waves rocked the boat gently up and down while Mark waited impatiently for Dave to return to the ship. Six months now they had been trapped in the past, and it was driving him crazy.

Sally was pregnant. He was sure of it.

He'd been hearing her voice off and on since they'd arrived back in the past. The only other times he'd ever heard her so clearly was when she had been pregnant with each of their daughters. It was yet another reason why he had to get home, and yet another reason why he felt as if he was slowly losing his mind from waiting.

That's all he had been doing, particularly for the last six weeks.

Waiting.

"Do you think he is good?" Rosalyn asked worriedly.

Her English had improved a lot since their arrival. She was scanning the calm water, her eyes wide with fear.

"Dave is good. Fine. Don't worry. He'll be back up in a couple of minutes," Mark tried to reassure her.

The boat they were on wasn't huge. That was one of the reasons why Rosalyn and her father alternated on who went out with Mark and Dave on what her father called their *loco quest*. He was still calling it that, despite the fact that Rosalyn was at this moment wearing a cord around her neck from which dangled an actual Spanish doubloon Dave had found in the water beneath their boat.

That had been five weeks ago, and it was why they were now on the water every single day searching for the Lita del Alma sterncastle. Mark was growing so impatient to find it and so desperate to get home that he no longer cared what part of the ship they found, as long as they found something which would help him buy his own boat so he could return to his wife.

If they screwed up history in the process, so be it. He just didn't want to continue being a part of that history.

"Have you got your camera working yet?" Rosalyn asked him.

"No, not quite," he admitted.

"You know, the cameras from this time are quite good," she said.

"I know, but this one is…special," he said with a shrug.

She glared at him, as she often did when she thought one of them was lying to her. A couple of months back, she'd managed to keep that glare going for a whole two days. That had been why Dave finally broke down and told her the truth.

To her credit, she took the whole time-traveler-from-the-future thing a heck of a lot better than he would have, given the same circumstances. Mark was just grateful she had believed Dave. Without her and her father's friendship, they'd be in a considerably worse predicament than the one in which they'd already found themselves.

He hadn't bothered explaining to her that the device he kept fiddling with was also a phone. Phones hadn't yet been invented and the less he had to explain to her the better. Every time he inadvertently told her something about the future, he worried about the potential consequences. At least Rosalyn and her father didn't seem like inventors who would jump on an idea and run with it. Then again, they didn't seem like treasure hunters, either, and yet that's exactly what he and Dave had gotten them involved in.

Rosalyn cried out as there was sudden movement in the water. Dave broke the surface a moment later with a gasp. He had been rigorously training himself to do free diving and he could now hold his breath for an impressive amount of time. Mark was training as well but was not nearly as advanced as Dave had become.

159

Dave held onto the side of the boat with his left hand as he treaded water and tried to catch his breath. He was grinning from ear-to-ear.

"I found it."

Mark started up from his seat, nearly dropping the phone he'd been futzing with. He caught it before it could hit the deck.

"Are you serious?"

Dave slowly pulled his clenched right hand out of the water. He held it up and then opened his fist to reveal a ruby an inch in diameter.

Rosalyn cried out in delight and Mark sputtered, trying to find the words. Tears filled his eyes, blurring his vision, and he quickly dashed them away.

In one moment, everything had changed. That one ruby Dave now clutched in his fist would be enough to get them a ship of their own.

No! A dozen ships.

They could go out as many times as they needed, lose ship after ship to storms and still have a ship when the storm they were searching for finally came.

Rosalyn was so excited she leaned over the side of the boat, grabbed Dave's head in her hands and kissed him right on the lips.

Dave was so startled he almost dropped the ruby.

Blushing a pretty pink, Rosalyn let go of Dave and retreated to the bow of the boat, leaving room for Dave to come aboard. Mark smirked as he stared at his friend, who looked far more overwhelmed by the kiss than by the ruby in his fist.

~

A few minutes later Mark was on his way down to the wreckage. He swam slowly for a few seconds close to the sea floor looking for the heap of twisted metal Dave had described. When he finally found it, his heart started pounding as he slowly reached down and picked up a fistful of doubloons which were spilling out of a hole gouged in the side. He could feel the metal in his fingers and could see it with his eyes through the haze, but it was nearly impossible to believe nonetheless. Like most little boys, he'd dreamed of finding buried treasure, but never in his wildest dreams had he ever thought it was actually possible.

Yet here he was, underwater with a fistful of gold coins.

It was going to take them weeks to bring all the treasure to the surface. His heart cried out against the delay. All he wanted to do was take the ruby, acquire a small armada and chase down the storm that would send him back home. As far as he was concerned, Rosalyn and her father could have the rest.

He had to be practical, though. He didn't know how much time and resources the pursuit of returning home was going to require. They couldn't afford to just abandon this discovery.

Besides, finding it again in a few weeks or months might not be that easy. As it was, they had discovered the sterncastle a good distance away from where Dave had thought they might find it. It was almost a mile from where the rest of the ship would be discovered in a few years.

Plus, they owed it to Rosalyn and her father to rescue as much of the treasure as they could. The two hadn't been obligated to help them, especially given their crazy story, and yet they had. Their kindness should not go unrewarded-- although given the way Rosalyn gazed at Dave and with the kiss she'd planted on him earlier, he was pretty certain what she was looking for had nothing to do with money.

~

Later that night, Mark finally completed the project he'd been working on in his spare time. It had taken a lot of effort, but he found a way to charge his smartphone. It was crude and he risked something going wrong and frying his phone altogether, but at least for now he had his pictures and several old voicemails from Sally to enjoy. Even more important than

161

that, he had a way to capture life here for Sally in case he didn't make it home. His first new picture was a selfie of himself with Dave, Rosalyn, the doubloons and the ruby.

"We have the money now. We should get our own place." Dave spoke up suddenly.

Mark's gaze snapped to Dave's. It was late and he had thought his friend was asleep.

"What? Why?"

"We've imposed on Rosalyn and her father long enough."

"With any luck, we won't be imposing that much longer," Mark said. "And we'll definitely be leaving them better than we found them."

"Still, it's unseemly for us to stay. We're not even relatives, and this is 1880. I'm surprised people haven't already started talking."

"Is this about the kiss?" Mark asked, sitting up and rubbing his eyes.

"No," Dave said a little too loudly.

"That's exactly what I thought. I get it. You don't want to live in the same house as your girlfriend."

"She's not my girlfriend!" Dave said, not at all amused.

"Just keep telling yourself that," Mark teased.

23

Mark awoke and sat up abruptly. It was a big day and joy and grief mixed within him in equal measure. It had been two years to the day that they had been trapped in the past. So much had happened in that time. They had found the sterncastle of the Lita del Alma, and after many painstaking dives, they had recovered enough gold and jewels to make them wealthy beyond measure.

They had ventured into the triangle trying to get back home more than two dozen times since then, had completely wrecked fifteen boats in the process and had broken twenty bones between them. Their brushes with death were beginning to take their toll both mentally and physically on each of the men. The locals thought they were crazy, but it turned out when you had enough money, people would limit the whispering to behind your back.

He knew his darling wife had a healthy baby boy, but the moment she delivered, he had lost the connection, just as he had with her two previous pregnancies. It had been fifteen months since he'd been able to feel her with him and it was slowly breaking his heart.

He took a deep breath. While there was grief to spare on this day especially, it was time to focus on the joy. Rosalyn had proven to be a savvy business partner and had risen to the challenge that was David. The priest had finally broken down and admitted the truth to her. The *whole* truth. Instead of running away, she had believed him and redoubled her efforts to change her beloved's life forever.

Today, they were getting married.

He had never seen his friend so happy or so befuddled. It

was as if Dave didn't know what to do with himself. Mark couldn't blame him. The possibility of marriage had never even entered the other man's mind before and now he was marrying a lady from a completely different time period.

In his own time he would have remained happily married to the Church. Here, however, he'd found a different destiny. Rosalyn was his match in every way. She was smarter than Dave, and as soon as he taught her to read, she was well on her way to becoming more educated than either of them. On more than one occasion, Dave had remarked that he'd created a monster, particularly when she debated him on theology or philosophy.

Mark got dressed in his best clothes as quickly as he could and then hurried to Dave's room. The two of them had bought a house together, but after today it was going to belong to Dave and Rosalyn, and Mark was going to find a place of his own. The newlyweds certainly didn't need a third wheel under their roof. Given the way that Rosalyn looked at Dave, Mark would be surprised if she even let him out of the bedroom for the first month.

Dave turned out to be a total wreck. He was wildly pacing his room like a caged tiger, one shoe on, one shoe off.

"You misbuttoned your shirt," Mark pointed out.

Dave swore in Latin. "This is the fourth time!"

"Here, let me help," Mark said. He rebuttoned the top button correctly. "There, now just work your way down. And you might want to try breathing once in a while."

His friend met and held his gaze. "What am I doing?"

"Getting married."

"I can't get married," Dave protested.

"Why not? I thought we settled the whole priest issue. I seem to remember a lot of discussion about God, and doors closing, windows opening. I think you even had a mental breakdown and started quoting Luther or something."

"I did no such thing!" Dave protested hotly.

"Well, that's my story, and I'm sticking to it."

"I'm not from here."

"I know. You're from Miami."

"You know what I mean!" Dave snapped, exasperated.

"Oh, the whole *you're from the future* thing? Well, if she's willing to accept it, then you should, too."

"But how can I take her back with me?"

"Simple. You load her up into the boat, get her one of those cork jackets, and when we actually make it home, you immediately take her to Walt Disney World and blow her mind."

"I'm being serious."

"So am I," Mark said. "Someone from the 1800s will be shocked not only at the thought of a theme park, but also at the fact that the entire world worships a mouse."

"How can I risk her life in those storms?"

And there they had it.

That one notion Mark had been thinking about for weeks. And he already knew the answer. He'd known for some time.

Dave couldn't go back.

Only his friend hadn't quite realized that yet. It appeared he was about to, though. It would hurt Mark to be so brutally honest with his friend, but the fact was that Dave loved Rosalyn just as much as Mark loved Sally. He couldn't let him throw that away, no matter the reason—even for him.

Because love was everything.

"Dave, we'll have plenty of time to work that out after the honeymoon."

Dave sat down on his bed and dropped his head in his hands. "What am I going to do?"

"Please don't tell me you need me to give you *the talk*, because that's just going to be awkward for both of us."

Dave made a face at him. Then he sighed, his expression growing serious. "Am I making a mistake?"

Mark looked him straight in the eyes. "No. Marrying Rosalyn is the single best thing you've ever done in your life. It's the right thing."

165

"Thank you," Dave whispered.

"That's what the Best Man is for."

"You are the Best Man."

"Of course I am," Mark said.

"No, you really are. You're the best man I have ever met."

"You're just saying that because I'm going to keep you from fainting at the wedding."

"I'm saying that because you have kept it together better than anyone else would have in your situation. I'm only just starting to understand what it's been like for you to be away from Sally for this long. How your heart must be breaking with every second you're apart."

Mark looked away. "Don't make me cry. If you make me cry then I'll make you cry and things will just get ugly."

"Okay. No crying. Check. Anything else?"

"Yeah. Finish buttoning up that shirt. We need to get you to the church on time."

~

The wedding was beautiful and the reception afterward was wild. Dave had spent a small fortune making sure it was the most memorable party anyone had ever seen. Of course, he and Rosalyn barely ate, didn't even notice the entertainment and were only marginally aware of their guests. They kept dancing together, staring dreamily into each other's eyes.

Finally, toward the end of the evening, Rosalyn started making the rounds with their guests and Dave stopped and stood by Mark for a moment. Dave was staring at Rosalyn and smirking in a way Mark had never seen him smirk before.

He had to ask.

"What are you thinking about right now?" Mark asked.

"My wife."

"Must be nice to be married."

"It is, and hopefully, especially for the reason I'm thinking about right now."

"Pervert," Mark said, trying not to laugh.

"Prude."

Mark hugged Dave. "I'm proud of you, man."

"Thank you for being here. Thank you for getting me here."

"You're welcome."

Moments later, Dave and Rosalyn departed arm-in-arm. Mark envied them, starting off their lives together. He remembered the feeling all too well. They were embarking on a brand new journey.

And he was hoping to embark on an old one.

Later that night, he took out the boat by himself, even knowing how incredibly foolish it was to go it alone. He was well aware this might be it for him. If he didn't make it home this time, he might not make it at all.

He kept wondering if there was a plan in all this, if they had been meant to be here so that Dave and Rosalyn could meet each other. If that was the case, then maybe he would be allowed to go home to his own family now.

He stayed out on the water for sixteen days, until he ran out of food and water. By the time he sailed back toward the port he was almost out of hope. He had avoided putting down any kind of roots here, but he realized he was going to have to, in case he never made it home.

St. Augustine was about to change in a big way. In a year Henry Flagler would arrive to spend the winter. When he did Mark would make sure to meet him and help nudge along Flagler's ideas about developing the town into a winter getaway for the wealthy. Then when Flagler started building his hotels a few years later, Mark should be able to work things so that he was an onsite consultant or manager for Carrère and Hastings, the architectural firm Flagler was going to be using.

Once in port, Mark began to walk. He hadn't secured accommodations because he'd been hoping it wouldn't come to that. Now he realized he should have prepared better. He was going to have to find someplace new to live. He was also going to have to make some more permanent plans in case he never made it back.

He thought of Sally and just how worried and heartbroken she must be, raising three children alone. In some ways, it had to be even worse for her, since she wouldn't know what had happened to him.

Did she believe he was dead? Had she gone on with her life?

Somehow, he didn't think so. Maybe it was the way they'd communicated when she was pregnant. But somehow, he just knew she was waiting.

Like a lightning bolt striking, a thought occurred to him and he came to a sudden stop. He thought about some of the time travel movies he'd seen.

What if there was a way to send her a message, letting her know he was still alive? If he did this right, he could get it to her right about the time he disappeared so she would know that he was desperately trying to get back to her.

Excitement welled inside him. Up until that point he had been walking aimlessly, but now he looked up. He was standing in front of a large stretch of empty land, and he realized with a start that he knew what was going to be on that piece of land in the future.

He smiled.

24

Mark opened his eyes slowly.

Today was the day.

There was something different. He could feel it in his bones. But rather than being elated, he felt a sense of foreboding. He sat up and grabbed the journal off his bedside table. With any luck, this would be the last time he had to write in it and tomorrow morning he'd be waking up next to his beloved wife.

He took extra care when shaving, wanting his skin to be as smooth as possible. Sally didn't like stubble because she said it was scratchy. He wondered if she would even recognize him. Ten years had given him a light dusting of grey hair and his face was more deeply tanned than she'd ever seen it.

In truth, he felt that he looked even older than he was. Life in the past was harsher in some ways, and he noticed Dave also seemed to be aging at a slightly accelerated rate. Still, they looked and felt much better than their peers of a similar age.

He couldn't help but wonder what would happen when he made it back. Would the Triangle spit him out roughly around the time he had left? Or would it spit him out ten years later, so that the same amount of time would have passed for both of them?

His stomach clenched at the thought. He would never wish that upon her. He also had no idea if his contingency plan would have been actually set into motion. What if she had moved or married someone else? What if he couldn't find her or she was unwilling to take him back? What if she was dead?

These and a thousand other questions plagued him until his gut was clenched so tight he could barely breathe. The future was completely unknown, and it scared him. He followed his plan, however, because the thought of doing nothing, of dying here in the past and never making it back to at least see Sally once again scared him even more than something else going wrong.

"I'm coming, Baby," he whispered as he turned away from the mirror.

A half an hour later, he was making the ship ready for sail. He heard a creak as someone else stepped on board. He turned around to see Dave with a toddler on his hip. It was his youngest son, Abraham. Fatherhood really suited Dave, who had settled rather naturally into the role. Abraham looked even more like Dave than his older brothers. They all had inherited Dave's distinctive nose, but Abraham had also inherited his eyes and his bright, inquisitive mind.

"Where you going, Uncle Mark?" Abraham asked him, wide-eyed.

"I'm going back home," Mark told the youngster as he tousled his hair.

"You really think you're going to make it this time?" Dave asked.

"Air's different today, can you feel it?"

"I feel it, but I don't like it," Dave said. "You don't have to go, you know. There's people who love you here."

He could hear the apprehension and the sorrow in his friend's voice.

"And you don't have to stay," Mark said softly.

Dave shook his head. "You know I can't leave, just as much as I know you can't stay."

Abraham began to struggle and Dave set him down. The little boy climbed onto a seat and sat there looking immensely pleased with himself. Dave stared at him, a smile on his lips.

"You were right, you know. They're all my kids," he said.

"They all have your nose," Mark affirmed. "And every time I see one of them, I'll tell them they had the most amazing great-great grandfather in the whole world."

Dave nodded and the two men embraced. Mark didn't even

170

bother to try and check the tears that spilled freely down his cheeks. "I'm going to miss you, my brother," he said. After all they'd gone through together, they were closer than brothers, but he had no words to adequately explain how he felt.

"The law firm has everything ready for Sally when the time comes?"

Mark nodded.

"Don't worry, we'll keep passing down the secret so that when the time comes, she'll know you're trying to get back to her."

"Thank you," Mark said, his voice wavering as he struggled with his emotions. "When I get back, is there any message you want me to give anyone?" Mark finally asked.

Dave shook his head. "No, and if anyone asks, tell them I died heroically or something like that. Make up a good story."

"You have the most heroic story already."

"Yeah, but if you tell people something like that they'll lock you up in a mental institution and throw away the key."

"I know," Mark said with a sigh. "Marooned on an island, surviving off our wits will have to do."

"That will have to do."

"And the local wildlife gave you an epic funeral, fit for a king."

Dave laughed. "That would be something to see."

"Yes, wouldn't it, though? Dolphins accompanying your raft to sea before I shot it with a flaming arrow."

"Viking funeral? Why not!"

Mark paused a moment and sniffed before the tears started streaming down his face again. "Come with me."

Dave shook his head as a small sob escaped him. "You know I can't leave my family and my friends. This place has become home, more than anywhere else I've ever been."

"I love you, man."

"Love you, too. Now get out of here before we both start blubbering."

Mark nodded. "I think we already are."

171

"Come on, Abraham, it's time for Uncle Mark to go," Dave said, scooping up the boy. "Past time, actually," he said, staring at Mark and giving him a small smile.

"Hopefully even though I got a late start I'll still get there on time," Mark said.

"Godspeed your way my friend. My brother."

"Take care of yourself."

"And you," Dave said.

They stood for a moment, the achingly painful goodbye too impossible for words. Finally Dave turned and disembarked, hugging his son tightly to his chest.

Mark watched them go with a heavy heart. And in that moment, he realized the terrible truth.

For the first time in his life, he was truly alone. And it was very likely that he was about to die alone, as well.

~

Mark set sail. The ship was light and fast, the best that money could buy. It was a fitting chariot to sail him into heaven or hell, depending on which he found out on the sea. He had barely made it to open water when he got his first glimpse of the clouds starting to cover the sun. It was nine in the morning, but it was rapidly becoming as dark as a moonless night.

Electricity crackled in the air all around him. The faint scent of ozone suggested that lightning had already struck somewhere nearby, though he had seen no flash of light nor heard the boom of thunder. He kept going, even though his heart pounded in fear. As desperately as he wanted to make it back to Sally and the children, he knew there was a large possibility that in moments he would lose everything he had ever worked for or loved. He might even lose his own life.

The risk was worth it. As long as there was breath in his body, he would keep trying to get back to her. She was his angel, his light, his northern star. Without her, there was nothing. *He* was nothing, as these last ten years had proven.

172

With her, there was everything. At the end of the day, there was no choice to be made.

He had tried to be more prepared this time. He had packed the boat with a lot of food and emergency supplies. He was also carrying a small fortune in gold doubloons which would serve him well no matter what time period he ended up in. He'd even brought souvenirs for Sally and the children. That had actually been Dave's idea. The man had more parenting experience now than Mark had and he insisted Mark take home some trinkets, as if he had been on some long, extended business trip and had not been a castaway trapped in the past.

Forward in time, backward in time, shipwrecked and stranded--he had tried to prepare for every eventuality. At least, as best as anyone could prepare for such a thing. And if the worst should happen…well, he'd prepared for that, too.

At last he was where he wanted to be, which was, as near as he could tell, close to where he and Dave had been sucked back into time. At least it was, after years of discussion and debate, their best guess as to the exact location.

He lowered the sails, sat down, pulled his compass out of his pocket, checked it and then began watching the skies. Again the sick, chilling sensation he'd had that morning washed over him, leaving him shaking.

Something was wrong.

He tried to tell himself it was just the ocean and atmospheric conditions. He tried to tell himself it was because nature was out of balance thanks to a coming vortex, which was exactly what he was waiting for.

None of it helped.

Though ten years had passed, he still remembered the events of their fateful fishing trip with complete clarity. Some things simply couldn't be forgotten. He still had nightmares about it all and would wake up screaming.

The wind suddenly stopped. The boat no longer rocked and creaked to its buffeting. The waves had died down with no wind to ruffle them and the ocean was as still as glass. The air hung heavy around him, pressing in against him as though trying to smother him. Each breath became a struggle and he did his best to keep himself calm. Panicking would just make it worse.

He glanced down at the compass in his hand. The needle was oscillating slowly back and forth as though it couldn't find north. He sucked in his breath. For the last ten years that he'd been trying to get home, the compass had never behaved in that fashion. It had always been perfectly true north.

The fog descended without warning. It closed in around him until he could barely make out the compass, which started spinning wildly. The hair on the back of his neck stood on end and the scent of ozone became overpowering.

Here we go.

25

Sally had been reading through all of Dave's books, trying to find more information about what had happened to him and Mark. She also read everything she could find about him as an author. Apparently, he had married a woman named Rosalyn and had a great many children and grandchildren.

Huh. Who would have thought it?

She had just about finished reading the last of his books when her phone rang.

"Mrs. White?" a deep male voice asked.

"Yes, that's me."

"I'm Frank Howard of the Howard, Prescott, and Stein law firm here in St. Augustine. I'm contacting you on behalf of our firm. Some items have been left in care of our firm for you."

"Items? What items?" she asked.

She'd never heard of the law firm before. They didn't represent any of Mark's business interests.

"I'm still working through all of that. I apologize. We should have reached out to you sooner, but Mr. Prescott, who was in charge of handling these matters, passed away suddenly a couple of months ago. We're still sorting through all of his files and I wanted to contact you as soon as possible to let you know."

"Thank you."

"Would it be possible for you to come up here sometime in the next few days to go over everything? I'll be up to speed by that time and we can speak about it then."

"Um, yes, I believe I can."

"Fantastic. Shall we say Thursday at 11 a.m.?"

"Yes, that will be fine."

She wrote down the address he gave her and then hung up. She wondered what on earth they could have that belonged to her.

Maybe Mark took out a life insurance policy or something and never told me about it, she mused to herself.

She'd arrange for her parents to watch Emma and Jayne for one day. She planned to book an early morning flight to St. Augustine then fly back the same day so she wouldn't have to be away overnight.

~

By the time Thursday arrived, Sally's curiosity was overwhelming her. She was at the airport at 4:30 am. When she arrived in St. Augustine she rented a car and was at the attorney's office right on time. The secretary showed her right in and she soon found herself sitting across a desk form Mr. Howard. He was an older man with silver hair at his temples and a kindly gaze. He welcomed her warmly.

"Again, I would sincerely like to apologize on behalf of the entire firm. I've gone through all the files, and it appears that Chuck Prescott, one of the partners of the firm, was meant to contact you about six weeks ago. Unfortunately, he was in a car accident eight weeks ago and passed away. He was what we like to call old school, and it took us a while to decipher his personal notes and files. I am very sorry for any difficulty this may have caused."

"Can you please just tell me what all this is about?" she asked, wanting to get past the pleasantries and into finding out whatever it was Mark had left her. After all, she didn't have any relatives in this part of the state. It had to be something to do with Mark.

"Well, it appears a relative of yours somehow anticipated your…existence…and left a significant estate for you."

It was an odd way to phrase it, and his expression was a little bewildered.

"I don't understand."

"Neither do I," he admitted.

"Can you tell me what the estate is?"

"I think it's better if I show it to you, if that would be okay with you."

It all felt very mysterious, but something about the man seemed quite earnest.

"All right," she agreed.

"Great. We're going two blocks. Would you like to drive or walk?"

"Walk," she said.

He nodded, and three minutes later they were outside heading down the street.

"This is the oldest part of town," he said. "This law firm is actually the oldest in the state. It was founded by one of my ancestors and his business partner, who was Chuck's ancestor."

"That's a lot of history," she said, admiring the architecture of the buildings they walked by. "My husband and I used to come here for a weekend getaway every once in a while."

Memories flooded her. She and Mark had walked this street a dozen times.

"There's one house up here we always loved to look at," she said. "I always thought it helped inspire some of his architectural designs."

The truth was that when they were first married, they used to daydream about someday moving here and buying that house. They would make up stories about the people who lived there and what their lives were like. By the time they'd had enough money to even think about doing something like that, they'd both been well-established in their careers and lives in Miami.

They crossed the street. Halfway up the block, she slowed as the house came into view. It tugged at her heart as all the memories of their daydreams came flooding back to her.

"Here we are," Frank said, stopping in front of the house.

"Here we are what?" she asked.

He gestured to the house. "This is yours."

"Excuse me?" she said, sure she hadn't heard him right.

"This house was willed to you."

"*This* house?"

"Yes."

"This house was willed to me?"

"Yes, Mrs. White, it was."

She stared at him in disbelief. "By whom?"

"The house's builder and original owner."

"What? How is that possible? I thought this house was really old."

"One hundred and fifty years old."

"Then how could this have been willed to me?"

"That is one of many mysteries surrounding this entire transaction. Why don't we discuss it inside," he said.

He produced a key from his pocket/ He unlocked the entrance gate and she followed him up the steps to the front door. He unlocked it and they went inside. The foyer was beautiful, with polished marble everywhere. He closed the door and then led her into a formal living room. All of the furniture in it was antique and looked as if it was the original furniture in the house.

He motioned her to a seat on one of the chairs and took a seat himself. He laced his fingers together and leaned forward.

"As I understand it, in September 1877, the owner of this house sat down with his attorney, the original Mr. Prescott, and made his final arrangements. He revealed to William Prescott that he was going to be taking a voyage and was concerned about what would happen if he didn't make it back. He stipulated that his entire estate, including this house, was to go into trust for Sally White. Your birthdate and address were given. He told William something that is only referenced in the papers as the Secret of The Guardians. Whatever it was it convinced William to help him. He apparently passed the file and The Secret down to his son, who then passed it on to his son all the way down to Chuck. In his appointment book, Chuck

178

had written down Sally White – Secret of The Guardians on September 17th. It took us until a few days ago to find your file. He had it in a personal safe no one else in the office knew about."

"So what is the Secret of The Guardians?" Sally asked.

He shook his head. "I don't know. It looks like it was never written down, only passed on verbally. What I can give you is the deed to this house and ownership papers related to a number of other properties and bank accounts. There's also some papers that I'll be giving you."

Her mouth had gone completely dry and her heart was beating painfully fast. "The original owner, what was his name?"

"Mark Gregory White."

"That's my husband!" she gasped.

26

Sally was shaking from head to toe. It was Frank's turn to stare at her. "What do you mean he was your husband?"

"Mark Gregory White was my husband. He disappeared in the Bermuda Triangle a few weeks ago, on September 16th. His ship was named *The Guardians*."

Frank passed a hand over his face and muttered something under his breath.

"You don't believe me," she said.

"No, actually, I think I just might. I've seen some strange things in my time. But this... How many children do you have?"

"Two girls and I'm pregnant with our third child," she said.

"Come with me," he said, standing and walking toward the foyer.

He began to speak as they walked through the house. "Mark Gregory White's life was fairly well-documented for ten years. Nothing is known about him before he showed up in St. Augustine, rescued off a deserted island by a fisherman along with a friend of his who became a famous local author. Mark White never married, so when I was inventorying the house I found something that seemed rather strange to me."

He led her into a study with a large, carved desk. He stopped and pointed to a portrait on the wall. It was massive, at least five feet tall, of a family dressed all in mid-nineteenth century clothing.

"When you showed up in my office, I thought it was an uncanny coincidence, but now I'm thinking it's not," Frank said.

She stared up at the portrait. There were five people in it. There was Mark, Emma, Jayne, and her, and in her arms was a baby.

She sank to her knees, and as she hit the ground, she noticed the mosaic tile that dominated the floor in the room. It was two intertwined hearts, exactly like the two intertwined hearts Mark had made for their bedroom.

Mark had made it.

She knew it as surely as if he was standing there telling her it was him.

"Are you okay?"

She heard Frank's voice coming from what seemed like a great distance.

"My husband, he made all this. He made it for me. He's never coming home."

Frank frowned in concern. "I'll give you a few minutes. I'll be in the other room when you need me. I believe he left something for you in the desk."

She listened for Frank's footsteps to retreat before moving. She sat there shaking in the middle of the intertwined hearts. The house they'd always loved had been theirs all along.

She finally got up and made it to the desk, where she fell heavily into the chair. She stared ahead at the room. This was the view Mark would have seen for years.

How many years?

When had he died?

The questions began to burn within her, one followed by another.

How did he die?

Frank had said something about the desk. She opened the drawers but found nothing other than faded paper and some quill pens. Finally, the bottom door on the right revealed a safe. She stared at it for a moment. Then she slowly spun the dials, using their anniversary as the combination.

The lock clicked and she opened the door, which creaked from age and disuse. She reached inside and pulled out a very

181

old book. She set it carefully in the middle of the desk.

For a moment she just stared at it, fascinated. It mesmerized her so that she couldn't look away. It also terrified her. She didn't want to open it, but she knew that she had to.

She took a deep breath and opened the cover. There on the first page in Mark's handwriting was a simple message.

To my beloved, Sally, this is my account of everything I have done to get back to you. Forever yours, Mark.

She quickly wiped the tears from her eyes so that they wouldn't fall on the pages and mar them.

She turned to the next page.

January 4, 1867

Just writing that date is hard to do. It seems impossibly hard to believe that some horrific twist of fate has thrown Dave and I into the past. It is our hope that we might find a way back to our own time through an encounter with a similar storm. Truth be told, we don't know if it was the storm or the fog or which of the supernatural elements we encountered were the actual cause of our time-traveling. We don't even know if we can get the phenomenon to repeat, whether it would even put us back in our own time or just throw us even farther back into the past.

We must try.

Dave's foot is healing from the break. He is almost well. As soon as he is, we will borrow a boat and head back out onto the sea.

January 23, 1867

The storm we encountered was horrific, but just a normal storm. Our boat was smashed to bits and Dave saved my life. We agreed that we have to acquire money to fund our expeditions, as we don't know how long it will take to encounter the anomaly again, and we're fairly certain no one else around here is likely to lend us another boat.

I can't express my anguish over being parted from Sally, Emma, Jayne, and the baby. Sally is pregnant. I can feel it. I can feel *her*. The only other times this has happened were when she was pregnant with Emma and Jayne. That's why I'm so certain. It kills me that I'm not there with all of them. I swear when I make it back I'll never leave Sally's side again, not even for an hour.

The pages went on and on, hundreds of them. Some had sketches and snatches of poetry. Many had the intertwined hearts on corners. She would go through it all later, cherish every word written. Now, though, she had to know. She flipped to the last entry.

December 12, 1879

I'm going out today to find the storm that will send me home. It grieves me that Dave can't go with me, but he will not leave his family. I understand that feeling all too well.

My heart is heavy this morning. I feel as though a shadow has fallen over me. As they say, I feel like someone just walked over my grave. I find myself afraid to go, but I know I must. Whether I go home or to the watery depths, I must try. I have never before felt this way.

In case I die, I am meeting with my attorney this morning to make final arrangements. I only hope Sally can someday forgive me for not making it back.

I will make it back, or I will die trying.

That was the last entry. She buried her head in her hands and wept openly.

After what seemed a very long time, she stood and made her way back to the sitting room, where she found Frank patiently waiting for her. He gave her a pained smile as he pulled an envelope from his jacket.

"There were instructions that I should give this to you," he said.

She took the envelope. Inside was a smaller, sealed envelope and a newspaper article from December 18, 1879. She read the article quickly. It announced the death of Mark White, tycoon and architect, who had been lost at sea. His boat had been caught in a storm. Some of the wreckage had been recovered.

He had been right. The storm had killed him. Grief filled her, but also a sense of peace. At last now she knew what had happened to him. As terrible as it was, the not knowing had been worse, in its own way. Now she could go home, hold a funeral and mourn him properly.

She turned her attention to the small envelope. She opened it and instantly recognized Mark's handwriting.

My Darling Sally,

It was my hope to show you my life here in the past and all the things I've done for you and the children. If you are reading this, it means I have failed to find my way home. Please know that I have always loved you, and everything I have done for the past ten years has been for you, the girls, and our baby boy who has yet to be born.

She stopped and reread the last sentence. He said she was having a boy. He *knew*. Somehow, he knew something she didn't yet know. The girls would be so excited to find out, since they wanted a baby brother. She continued reading.

> *There is a coral cave on the grounds of this property with a waterfall. I built that for you. I built so many things in this town for you and our children. Please tell them I love them and thought about them every hour of every day. I would have given everything to see them grow up.*
>
> *There are a number of investments that the attorney will tell you about. I left something special for you behind the waterfall, though. Reach in and pull on the sharp rock. You will know what to do after that.*
>
> *I love you with all my heart. I always have. I always will. In this time and in every time. I remain your loving "favorite husband."*

She couldn't help but smile. It was an old joke between them. She would call him her favorite husband sometimes, just to tease him. She took a deep breath. No one but him could have written that note.

He had signed his name, and she ran her finger over it. She cleared her throat and looked up. "He mentions a coral cave on the property."

"Yes, I can take you there," Frank said.

"Actually, if you can just point me in the right direction, I'd like to go by myself."

"Certainly. I have a number of other documents and things to give you at the office. How about you join me there when you're done here?"

"Thank you. That would be fine," she said.

He nodded and handed her the key.

"The grounds here include a fifteen-acre garden. You'll find the coral cave with the waterfall in the dead center, surrounded by a circle of palm trees."

She nodded and took the key.

He left, closing the front door behind him.

She wandered through the house for a few minutes, noticing every room had the two intertwined hearts as an architectural accent somewhere within the space. There were more pictures he'd had painted of her and the girls. She even found a purple tulip pattern in the china on display in the dining room.

After some time, she was finally ready to leave the house and explore the cave. She strolled into the gardens and to the circle of palm trees. There, in the heart of them, was the waterfall with the cave. It was a small waterfall, though very beautiful. She reached in, felt for the sharp stone and pulled.

The waterfall parted suddenly, revealing a combination lock built into the stone. She had to walk around to get to the lock. Once again, she used their anniversary as the combination. There was a groaning clunk that lasted a few seconds and then the stone parted in the middle, revealing a chamber inside. She had to pull hard on the door to fully open it. She stepped in and was overwhelmed by what she saw. All around her was treasure. There were gold plates and goblets, chests filled with large gemstones and others filled with gold coins. Mark had left her a literal treasure trove.

She gasped as she saw the paintings and recognized some of them from Art History classes she had taken in college. Rembrandt, Rubens, and so many others. She stared, dumbstruck, wondering how Mark had possibly gotten hold of them. The art collection alone had to be worth hundreds of millions of dollars.

Her heart swelled. Even in hardship, Mark's thoughts had been for her and their children. It was as though he was reaching out and caring for her beyond the grave.

As she turned to leave, her eyes fell on a pedestal. There, sitting in an exalted position amongst so many amazing treasures, was something which meant more to her than anything that glittered in that vault.

She reached out a shaking hand and picked up Mark's phone. Her hand wrapped tight around it. There were pictures, memories stored in there. She held it to her heart for a moment and then slipped it into her pocket. She'd look at it later, when she was somewhere she could spend the time and the tears.

She closed up the vault and moved the stone trigger back into position. The waterfall started back up and even she couldn't tell what secrets were hidden behind it.

She began to walk the gardens, seeing Mark's touch everywhere she looked. After a few minutes, she heard singing. She followed the sound and discovered a woman her age placing fresh bouquets of flowers in front of two marble gravestones.

"Hello?" Sally called out tentatively.

The woman turned, startled. "What are you doing--"

She stopped in mid-sentence and her eyes grew wider. She starred at Sally in disbelief for a few seconds then took a step toward her. "It's you, isn't it?"

"Excuse me?" Sally asked, wondering how the woman thought she knew her.

"You're Sally White. You're great-uncle Mark's wife."

She turned and indicated the stone monument behind her. Sally stepped forward until she could read the name inscribed.

Mark White

Beneath it was written,

Beloved Husband, Father, and Brother.

On the gravestone next to his was written,

David Lawrence Whitcomb

Beloved Father, Grandfather, Great-Grandfather.

Sally's hand flew to her mouth, stifling the scream that came to her lips.

She was staring at Mark's and Dave's graves.

"I'm sorry. This must be terribly hard for you. It's just that I've been waiting to meet you all my life," the other woman said with a gentle smile.

"Who are you?" Sally asked.

"I'm Kayla Whitcomb. Dave was my great-great-great-great grandfather. Mark, your husband, was like a brother to him, and

187

an uncle to his children. So, in many ways, that makes you my aunt."

Sally just stared at her incredulously. "You know?"

Kayla took a deep breath. "Yes. Our family knows the secret, although we've keep it very hush-hush so no one thinks we're crazy. We've been waiting for the day we finally got to meet you. There were so many stories handed down in the family about you and Uncle Mark and Emma and Jayne. And, if I'm not mistaken, you're pregnant with a little boy."

"I guess so," Sally said.

Sally spontaneously threw her arms around Kayla.

The other woman hugged her back, holding her tight.

"Welcome home," she whispered.

~

On a beach, a bedraggled man opened his eyes. His clothes were in tatters and still wet from the sea. Every bone in his body hurt. His ears were ringing and his head was spinning. He spit the sand out of his mouth and pushed himself slowly to his knees as his memories came flooding back to him.

The fog had come, and then the blackness and the storm. He stood to his feet, his knees shaking and nearly refusing to support his weight. He gazed around, struggling to see some kind of landmark, hoping to find anything that he could recognize. All he saw was beach in both directions without a soul on it.

He coughed, spitting up more salt mixed with seawater. When he could catch his breath, he straightened up fully.

"Now, when the hell am I?" Mark said.

Epilogue

Present Day

Sally was running late for the museum gala. She had loaned a couple of the paintings Mark had collected for her to the institution for a new exhibit. Tonight was the official unveiling and they expected her to make a speech. She was in the office rehearsing it.

"Purrty," Mark, Jr. said as he latched onto the hem of her purple dress.

"Thank you, honey," she said as she smiled down at him.

"Are we going to the party?" he asked.

"No, Auntie Kayla is going to be babysitting you and your sisters tonight."

The little boy grinned in delight.

Kayla had been such a godsend. Sally wasn't sure what she would have done without her. Six weeks after discovering that she owned the mansion she and Mark had always admired, she had packed up the girls, left Miami behind, and settled in.

The first year had been rough. Everywhere she looked she saw her husband's handiwork in the home he'd built for them. It made her miss him more just as his thoughtfulness made her love him more. Kayla had been there, a shoulder to cry on when she needed it. She had told and retold every old story she knew about Mark and Dave with extreme patience.

Indeed, the entire Whitcomb family had embraced her and the children. They really had made it feel like a homecoming.

She glanced down and saw that Mark, Jr.'s shoes were untied, as usual. She crouched down and began to tie them even as he squirmed.

"Knock, knock," she heard Kayla say as she entered the room. She sounded a little breathless as though she had been hurrying.

"I'm so glad you're here," Sally said without looking up.

"Me, too. I found someone outside who wanted to see you."

"Yeah? Who is it?" Sally asked.

A deep husky voice answered, "Your favorite husband, I hope."

Sally froze as her heart stopped for a moment. She recognized that voice. It was older, rougher, but it still made her feel warm inside.

She stood slowly, afraid to look up as her heart began to pound. What if she was wrong? She couldn't bear it. She took a deep, shuddering breath.

"Has he come to take me on a second honeymoon?" she asked.

"Paris, St. Augustine, wherever you want," the man's voice trembled with emotion.

She forced herself to look up and she gasped.

Mark was standing just inside the door. His hair was tinged with gray, his face was a little more weather-beaten and deeply tanned. His clothes hung in tatters off him and there were scrapes and bruises visible.

"Mark?" she asked, praying it wasn't some specter.

Mark, Jr. looked up at her, then at the man. "Daddy?" he asked. Suddenly the little boy ran to him.

Mark scooped his son up into his arms. "Hi, pal, I've been waiting for so long to meet you," he said.

It was like a dam inside her broke. Sally ran forward and threw her arms around both of them as she began to cry uncontrollably. A moment later Mark's lips were on hers and she closed her eyes as she kissed him back.

She didn't know how long they were that way, but she soon heard running footsteps.

"Daddy!" Emma and Jayne shrieked as they threw their

190

arms around his waist.

"My babies," he sobbed.

Sally looked at Kayla. The other woman was smiling through the tears streaking down her face.

Sally freed one arm and motioned to her. Kayla eagerly moved forward and hugged them all. "Welcome home, Uncle Mark," she said.

"Thank you. I can tell you're one of Dave's. You have his eyes."

Kayla nodded. "What happened to you after you left Great-Grandfather Dave?"

Mark gave her a short little laugh and then turned and stared deep into Sally's eyes. "Tonight is a night for celebrating. That story will just have to wait."

Made in the USA
Monee, IL
11 May 2020